A Home for Bella

A Home for Bella

A Heartwarming Novel of a Single Woman's
Dream and an Unforgettable Friend

MARY CASEY

Editor: Nina Shoroplova—NinaShoroplova.ca
Cover Designer: Pagatana Design Service—pagatana.com
Book Interior and E-book Designer: Amit Dey—amitdey2528@gmail.com
Production & Publishing Consultant: Geoff Affleck, AuthorPreneur
    Publishing Inc.—geoffaffleck.com

ISBN: 978-1-7399279-0-5 (Paperback)
ISBN: 978-1-7399279-1-2 (eBook)

FIC027020 FICTION / Romance / Contemporary
FIC044000 FICTION / Women
FIC066000 FICTION / Small Town & Rural
FIC106030 FICTION / World Literature / Ireland / 21st Century

This is a work of fiction inspired by real events. While many of the locations in the novel are real, all characters are fictitious.

Dedication

This novel is dedicated to my loving parents for all their kindness and for never charging me rent. To my amazing siblings and their partners for all their support. To my adorable nieces and nephews who bring joy and laughter to my life. To all my fabulous friends for always being there. To the memory of an unforgettable friend who taught me to have a grateful heart. To my loyal companion Lucy who sat at my feet while I wrote. To all my previous housemates that I have been blessed to live with. Finally I would like to dedicate this novel to anyone with a dream of purchasing a house. I believe in you. Follow your heart, be persistent, stay focused on your dream, and most of all be grateful.

Contents

CHAPTER 1

An appraisal

'Bella, dear, whatever is the matter with you? You seem so sad, lost and worried,' said Joan in a caring, soft voice.

Bella was lying in her bed alone in the dark. Tears were streaming down her face. Joan with her beautiful smile handed Bella a handkerchief. As Bella wiped away her tears, she could feel warm arms wrap softly around her. For that brief moment, she felt safe and loved. A bright light filled the room, followed by a large bang that woke Bella up suddenly from her dream.

It's okay, it's just the bin men, she thought. The bang was followed by the sounds of bin men chatting and clattering bins. *Oh crap!* She suddenly realised it was Monday again, which meant work. Bella had hated Mondays for as long as she could remember. Weekends just seemed to go by so quickly. She looked over at the clock on her bedside table and was delighted to see she had another ten minutes before the alarm would sound.

Bring in the four-day week, I am begging you, God.

As Bella thought of the day ahead, she could feel a knot in her stomach—today was her dreaded annual performance appraisal with Ruth. In her sales role, Bella was responsible for selling HR software products to other companies. She loved working as a sales account rep. She was gaining a lot of valuable knowledge and experience working for this innovative multinational company. She liked how the company was always investing in training for their employees and was focused on career development. The office was modern and comfortable and the building got a lot of natural light. Bella loved the vibrant colours used in the interior of the office. The food and coffee in the cafeteria was amazing too.

Bella's only problem with work was her manager Ruth. Bella could not warm to her. Ruth was just so demanding and was forever on Bella's case. She felt that Ruth did not encourage her or recognise her for her hard work, and as a result, she felt unmotivated. Bella found it so difficult to have a conversation with her manager. She avoided Ruth in the office whenever possible.

Bella had worried herself all weekend, thinking about her appraisal; she knew it was not going to go well.

The alarm sounded, and she dragged herself out of bed. After ten minutes of looking through her wardrobe, she finally found her black pencil skirt and white silk blouse. *I knew they had to be here,* she thought, feeling relieved.

All I need now are my black high heels. And she crawled under her bed to get them. She went to the kitchen and pulled out the ironing board. Bella hated ironing and would only iron when it was absolutely necessary. She would try to buy clothes that didn't tend to crease easily. She wondered how her friend Joan had ironed her own and the O'Sullivans' underwear when she was lending a hand to Bella's mum. It just seemed like a crazy thing to do. Joan always said to Bella she loved ironing; she found it therapeutic. It was an opportunity for her to reflect on her day and see where she needed to take action in her life and experience more joy.

Dressed now and with her face made up to hide the dark circles under her eyes, Bella grabbed her handbag and car keys from her bedside table. She never had time for breakfast. She was always running late and in a panic. Bella was only a ten-minute drive from the office, but some mornings with heavy traffic in town she could be nearly an hour getting to the office. Today was one of those mornings in the west of Ireland as rain was pouring down from the heavens. Bella would use her commute time to listen to her favourite music, but this morning the music was just not helping. She could not shake the negative mood she found herself in.

On arriving at work, she saw Mark going into the elevator. He held the elevator door open for her. 'Thanks,

Mark. I nearly missed it,' she said smiling. Just his presence seemed to cheer Bella up.

'How was the weekend, Bella?'

'Busy. I was out all weekend again. I am wrecked now and still recovering,' she replied. 'Yours? Did you get up to much?'

'No, I just went hiking at the weekend with Tracey. The weather was fabulous, wasn't it?'

Bella had met Tracey at the work Christmas party last year. Ruth had decided it would be a good idea to invite all partners to the party. Everyone had brought someone, except for Bella who entered the restaurant solo. In case anyone hadn't known Bella was single, they discovered it at the party. Bella hated being single for Christmas; couples just seemed so happy and loved up.

'It was a nice change to see the sun,' said Bella. 'Rain again this morning.' Just hearing Tracey's name made Bella feel jealous. Mark was the perfect guy. He was handsome, athletic, and he was a pure gentleman. Bella longed to find someone like Mark.

They got out of the elevator. Bella walked swiftly to her desk noticing on the wall clock it was 9.15am. She was late again and it was becoming a habit.

Emma was sitting at the desk next to hers. She smiled up at Bella and continued to speak on the phone. Bella logged in to her computer and started the day. Bella had trained Emma when she had first started with the company five years ago, and their friendship had blossomed. Bella thought Emma always looked like she had just stepped out from a beautician's. Her make-up was flawless, her nails at all times were manicured and painted. Her trendy short black bob perfectly styled, and she never seemed to have a bad hair day.

Emma was due to get married this year at Christmas. She had met her partner Dave on Tinder and after two months of dating, she moved into Dave's house. Six months later they were engaged. Emma had come to work one day with a rock on her finger, and Bella had noticed it sparkling straightaway.

Even though Bella was happy for Emma, it just seemed to Bella that all her friends now were either buying houses, getting engaged, getting married or announcing they were pregnant. Everyone except for Bella seemed to have news or be celebrating something. She longed to find her soulmate, purchase a house and settle down, but it just was not happening for her.

Bella was feeling pressure build up inside her, and she was stressing out about her current circumstances. Bella knew the qualities she wanted in a man, but she just could not find him.

Due to past experiences, Bella had developed a very negative mindset toward romantic relationships. She felt she had no luck with men. Bella thought back to her prom.

At 18, Bella had been a very quiet and shy girl who never had a boyfriend. Bella had summoned up the courage to ask Richard, her friend's brother to the prom. Bella was delighted when Richard said he would be honoured to go with her as she secretly had a mad crush on him.

On the evening of the prom, when Bella had just finished getting ready, she received a call from Richard. He was sick and, unfortunately, he could not go with her. Bella was gutted. How could she go now and be the only girl there without a date? She would look pathetic.

'You have to go,' said Bella's mum. 'It's your prom. You are all dressed up now and I have done your hair and makeup. You look stunning.' Bella wore a red, off-the-shoulder, floor-length chiffon evening dress specially made for the prom.

She was too upset to respond.

Now she was sitting on her bed sobbing and disappointed. Bella thought Richard just didn't want to go with her, and him feeling unwell was just an excuse. Bella was so critical of herself and always thought the worst. Her plan was to throw herself a pity party.

Bella wasn't going to go to her prom until Joan called in. Joan was an elegant, petite lady who lived nearby, an older woman who had embraced her silver hair. Since the age of three, Bella had known Joan. Joan had minded Bella and her siblings when the O'Sullivan parents were at work. Bella loved Joan's enthusiastic attitude to life; she always seemed to be so happy and had such a positive energy about her. It didn't matter what day of the week it was, what problem Joan faced, she just chose to be happy. Bella had never met anyone quite like her.

Bella looked up to Joan and she loved hearing her wise words guiding her through life. Joan was always cheering Bella on. Now at seventy five, Joan never cared what people thought of her, and Bella loved that about her. On all occasions Joan was dressed immaculately. Her house was always in order, and she used to say to Bella that this helped her keep her mind in order.

There was a little knock on Bella's bedroom door. 'Please come out, from your room, Bella,' said Joan. 'I want to see you wearing your dress.'

'I am not going,' answered Bella from inside.

'Please yourself,' said Joan, 'but I still want to see your dress on you. Come on, please.'

Bella opened her bedroom door slowly, and Joan walked in smiling.

'Oh, Sweetie, you look absolutely gorgeous. Bella, you are like a model.'

Bella blushed.

'Well, apart from that mascara all over your cheeks,' added her mum.

'That's an easy fix,' said Joan smiling. 'We've all been through that.' Joan handed Bella a small box of chocolates, and a single yellow rose she had picked from her garden. Bella smiled as she knew she could rely on Joan to cheer her up and lift her spirits.

Joan could also be very blunt with Bella when she needed to be.

'Now come on, Bella, don't be so ridiculous,' said Joan. 'If I had to wait for a guy before I would go anywhere or do anything, I would have spent my life waiting. Stop waiting for a man, Bella, or you will miss out on life. You will only get to go to one prom and you will regret it if you do not go. Trust me. Life is short, so get up and go and have fun.

'Bella, be grateful you are not the one who is sick,' said Joan. 'You have two options here: sit on your bed and be miserable all night, which I guarantee you will be, or get up and go and you can create an amazing night for yourself. We may not love our circumstances in life, and sometimes our plans don't work out, but that's life, and you just need to get on with it.'

'Okay, okay. I'll go,' said Bella, and she got up from her bed. Bella's mum and Joan said they would drop her off at the bus.

'Have a good night, Bella,' said her mum as Bella left the car. Bella's mum was relieved to see her get on the bus.

'Thanks, Joan, for persuading her to go. She wasn't listening to me at all.'

'I know. The poor thing,' said Joan. 'I did feel so sorry for her, all dressed up and sobbing. I am sure though he won't be the last guy to break her heart.'

Bella's mum agreed.

On the bus, a tall guy dressed smartly in a navy suit asked Bella if he could sit beside her. She and Adam got chatting, and Bella was relieved to find out that Adam was also going to the prom by himself as he had been dumped two weeks previously by his girlfriend for 'being too nice'. To Bella's surprise, she had an amazing night at her prom and, as usual, Joan knew best.

Emma's voice brought Bella back from her thoughts. 'Fancy lunch out today? I need a change from the cafeteria.'

'Yes, why not? Let's treat ourselves,' said Bella.

They got their coats and umbrellas and headed out to Murphy's. It was a cosy little bar serving home-cooked meals. As they entered, they could smell the aromas. Bella hated cooking, so most days she would eat out or have her dinner in the cafeteria. They sat down beside the fireplace and ordered.

'Bella, I love that pencil skirt on you. You look so stylish,' said Emma.

'Thanks, I am running out of clean clothes at this stage,' said Bella.

'Has the landlord not fixed the washing machine yet?' asked Emma.

'No, and I have rung him five times about it. Then I received a text from him this morning to say he is putting up the rent. Oh, I just hate renting and having to deal with landlords!' said Bella, quite annoyed.

Their lunch hour soon passed, spent mostly with Emma telling Bella all about her wedding plans. Emma had gone wedding dress shopping, and she was so excited to be sharing all the details with Bella now that she had found THE dress. Bella had been honoured to be bridesmaid four times in the past, and she used to love going with the brides-to-be while they were trying on wedding dresses.

'The dress is just perfect,' Emma said. 'I really do feel like a princess wearing it.'

'Don't tell me any more about the dress! You will ruin my surprise when I see you,' said Bella.

'With eight months to the wedding, all I need to do now is lose a stone. Any chance you would like to go walking after work? I need someone to motivate me.'

Bella agreed immediately. She loved walking and would go for a walk most evenings after work to clear her head. Working in sales could be very stressful at times as there were targets to meet plus the added pressure from Ruth.

When they arrived back at the office, Bella sat down in the meeting room, fidgeting. Two minutes later, a curvy lady with short auburn hair entered the room just as Bella was rubbing lip balm into her chapped lips.

'How are you today, Bella?' asked Ruth.

'I'm fine,' replied Bella.

'I won't keep you too long,' said Ruth.

Bella thought she was so stern-looking, cold and intimidating. Most of the sales team were afraid of Ruth. Bella's palms were starting to sweat and her heart was pounding.

'Bella, I have reviewed your evaluation, and I have rated your performance as "needs improvement".'

Bella looked at Ruth's laptop and listened as Ruth went through her appraisal. Ruth then started with the negative feedback. 'I am afraid you will not be receiving a performance bonus this year, Bella. You need to bring in new clients and improve on your cold-calling skills and increase your revenue targets.'

Ruth kept on talking, but Bella stopped listening when she heard there would be no bonus. Bella had now started to focus on Ruth's gold locket as Ruth kept touching it as she spoke. Focusing on the locket distracted Bella from crying. She didn't want to appear weak to Ruth and she knew she would not be able to respond to her manager's feedback without getting emotional so she chose not to make her case. 'Okay,' was all Bella could muster as she started to get up from her chair.

'Bella, I just know you are capable of so much more, and I hope you really do take my feedback on board.'

Bella went back to her desk and could not hide her upset from Emma.

'Bella, are you okay? Come on, let's go for a cuppa.'

Bella told Emma that Ruth was not happy with her overall performance, and she was not getting a bonus. 'It's just not fair,' said Bella. 'Looks like I won't be climbing the corporate ladder either anytime soon.'

Bella was very passionate about her work, and at a recent team meeting, she had picked Ruth up on a mistake she had made. Now she felt Ruth had it in for her.

'Come on, Bella,' consoled Emma. 'Forget about Ruth; everyone knows what she is like. I didn't get a bonus this year either, don't be so hard on yourself. Don't pay any heed to her; you know you are good at selling, and that's evident by your results.'

Emma always seemed to put a positive spin on things. 'Stop focussing on the negative, Bella. It won't do you any good. It will just bring more negative energy your way and give you wrinkles.'

For a moment, Bella thought it was Joan speaking to her.

Bella felt better after the pep talk from Emma, but when she got home, she found herself still thinking about her appraisal. Her negative thoughts were toxic; she was her own worst critic. She went to bed early that night, but couldn't sleep. She was going over and over the meeting in her head. Bella had a tendency to do this when she had a problem, or what in her mind she perceived to be a problem.

Bella became annoyed at herself for letting her manager get to her so much. She was a constant worrier, and had become an expert at creating the worst possible scenario in her head. Thoughts of losing her job were now entering her mind.

Last week Bella had attended a health and wellness programme at work. The speaker had promoted the benefits of journaling, saying it helps to reduce stress and anxiety, boosts your mood, improves your confidence and helps you to be happy and grateful. Bella had thought of Joan during the course, as for years Joan had kept a journal by her bedside. Every night, Joan would write three things in her journal that she was grateful for. Joan would also send love to those who had annoyed her during the day.

'There will be plenty of people in this life who will annoy you, Bella,' Joan had said to her one day. 'You just have to learn not to give them any of your headspace—you are responsible for all your thoughts.'

Joan was always trying to convince Bella that she should give journaling a go, saying it would help her to count her blessings in life, but Bella had continually dismissed the idea ... until tonight. She turned on her bedroom light and walked over to her pink chest of drawers. She opened a drawer and took out a hardback notebook and wrote 'Bella's Journal' on the cover. As she began to write she realised that gratitude was going to help her become aware of the good things she currently had in her life. It might help her focus on positive emotions and attract more good into her life.

A few weeks passed, and Bella continued to write every night in her journal. She was now paying more attention to her thoughts. She noticed that she had been used to a lot of negative self-talk. 'No one loves me. No one cares. I'm not confident. I am useless. I am not worthy. I am not pretty enough. Why me?' These were phrases that plagued her.

Bella realised she needed to change this negative self-talk to positive self-talk. She started saying daily affirmations. These empowering positive statements would help her to reprogram her mind and stop thinking negatively. By saying them she would affirm what she wanted in her life and create it. Bella stuck these affirmations to her bedroom mirror as a reminder to repeat them every day. She knew she needed to make herself accountable to someone so she would stay on this new path of gratitude and affirmation. As Joan believed in journaling and Bella looked up to her, Bella decided she would be accountable to Joan.

Bella's awareness grew, and whenever she started to think negative thoughts or felt vulnerable, she would quickly repeat one of her positive affirmations. They were helping her to condition her mind with a positive attitude. Standing in front of a mirror, she would look into her eyes and say the phrases. The hardest one was, 'Bella O'Sullivan, I love you, and you are a confident, amazing and successful woman.'

Bella's entries in her journal

Three things I am grateful for

Murphy's for its home-cooked meals

My family

My friends

Joan's wise words to me

We may not love our circumstances in life and sometimes our plans don't work out but that's life and you just need to get on with it. Stop complaining.

Stop waiting for a man, Bella, or you'll miss out on life.

Always keep your home in order as it will help you keep your mind in order.

There will be plenty of people in this life who will annoy you; just learn not to give them any of your headspace. You are responsible for all your thoughts.

Give journaling a go as it will help you count your blessings in life.

Someone I need to send love to

I send love to Ruth for her negative feedback at my appraisal.

Positive affirmation

Bella O'Sullivan, I love you, and you are a confident, amazing and successful woman.

CHAPTER 2

A hangover from hell

*I*t was Bella's favourite day of the week—Friday. And this weekend was extra special as she was off work on Monday for the bank holiday. Bella had always considered the May bank holiday to be the official start of her summer.

'Morning, Emma. Happy Friday,' Bella said, dropping a chocolate muffin on Emma's desk.

Emma's eyes lit up. 'You really are a bad influence,' she said. 'What are we celebrating?'

'Nothing,' said Bella smiling. 'It's just a treat. Well, I suppose I am rewarding myself for exceeding my revenue targets this month.' Joan regularly said to Bella how important it was in life to celebrate the little wins as they will keep you motivated and increase your confidence.

'Well done! That's fantastic,' said Emma. 'That will keep Ruth off your back for a while.'

Bella was now thankful for Ruth's constructive feedback at her appraisal. Much to her surprise it had seemed to motivate her into action, once she got over her initial upset. Bella had written down all her negative thoughts about the appraisal on a piece of paper which she then burnt. She replaced the negative thoughts with positive ones and focused her attention on setting weekly objectives for herself at work. Joan faithfully practised this when she was thinking a negative thought about something that had happened or a problem she had.

As she drove home from the office that day, Bella felt giddy as she and her housemate Kate had invited their friends over to their apartment for dinner and drinks. They had planned to hit the town after.

When Bella arrived home, Kate was busy in the kitchen preparing dinner. Kate had long blonde hair and everyone described her as beautiful. She also had a dazzling personality. Bella admired Kate as she knew how to have fun and was just so adventurous.

'How is the curry looking?' said Bella. 'It smells great. I'm starving.'

'It's almost done,' replied Kate.

'I'll set the table,' said Bella.

Two years earlier, Bella and Kate had moved into this two-bed modern apartment together. It was bright and comfortable but the best thing was it was located only five minutes from town. Bella was very fortunate over the years as she had been able to house share with her close friends. The thought of having to move into a house with strangers had always scared her.

Bella had known Kate since secondary school. Kate was also single and was enjoying her single life. Most weeks she would have a date lined up, and Bella thought her dating brought a bit of excitement to the apartment. There were a lot of weekends when Bella had planned to have a quiet weekend in, watching rom-coms, until Kate gently persuaded her to hit the town.

This evening they had invited Sarah, Amy and Laura over for dinner. They had met the girls in college. They didn't get to see the girls much now as they were all married with young kids to look after, so Bella and Kate were looking forward to the catch-up.

The doorbell rang, and the three friends arrived together.

'Love the dresses, girls, you all look fabulous,' Bella praised.

'You too,' said Amy. 'I love your silver sandals. They are so sparkly.'

'I don't know how you walk in them; they are so high,' observed Laura.

'Bella, you're so tall, without heels,' said Sarah. 'I'm in my comfortable kitten heels tonight but I am not out to impress.'

'Oh, just an old pair I've had for ages,' Bella told them. Bella was known for her shoe shopping. She was obsessed with buying shoes so she would quickly brush off any remarks made on them.

It was not long before they were all devouring the curry, sipping wine, chatting nonstop and laughing.

'Come on, girls,' said Bella. 'It's nearly ten. I'll order a taxi to town, or we will never leave the apartment.'

As Bella and Kate were single, they preferred to be drinking out in the bars rather than drinking in the apartment. They were constantly looking for the next opportunity to meet their princes. As the girls entered O'Connor's Bar, they could see it was wedged, and a queue had formed at the bar.

'Looks like town is going to be busy tonight,' said Bella.

The girls loved O'Connor's as it played live traditional Irish music, and there was always such a buzz. Bella squeezed her way toward the bar and got a round of drinks for everyone. As she brought down the drinks, she could see her friends had already started chatting to a group of men. Bella could not help noticing the men's arm muscles, with the tight t-shirts they were wearing. She gave the gin and tonics to her friends and winked at Kate who was chatting to a fair-haired, tanned man holding a pint of Guinness.

'Bella, meet Craig, Oliver and John,' said Kate. 'They are in Galway for the long weekend.'

Bella smiled, shaking hands with them all. The rest of the girls looked on as Kate and Bella chatted to John and Craig. Oliver moved on once he realised the other women were spoken for.

From Bella's scan of the men's fingers, they all appeared to be wearing no wedding bands. Bella habitually checked for rings and on a few occasions she had witnessed men take off their wedding rings in the bar. Bella hated to see this. She could not think of anything worse—the wife at home and the husband out pretending he was single.

Kate used to remind her that in today's society they might be in open relationships. That didn't interest Bella.

'So, where is the nightclub?' asked John.

'It's just across the road,' said Bella.

'Perfect. That's close,' said John. 'Are you and your friends going there tonight?'

'I don't think so,' explained Bella. 'We'll probably just stay here, not sure if my friends are up for clubbing.'

'So, you can come with me,' John said, smiling and staring into her eyes. 'I'll look after you.'

'No thanks, John. I'm going to stay with my friends.'

Bella knew John would persist. He had gorgeous blue eyes, and Bella was enjoying his company. She was trying not to appear too keen. Craig came back with a round of baby Guinness shots for everyone. After downing the shot, Bella went to powder her nose.

'God, she's hard work,' observed John to Craig. 'But, she is gorgeous. I love her chocolate brown eyes. Craig, we'll have to get the women to come to the nightclub with us.'

'So, Girls, should we hit the club?' Bella asked eagerly as soon as she came back.

From their expressions, she knew the only one that was up for going was Kate. And as they were all going to be staying in their apartment overnight, Bella didn't want to separate the group on their night out together. Bella was very loyal to her friends and she would never let a friend down, especially for a man she had just met.

Craig and Kate seemed to be getting on well, and he appeared to be funny, or maybe it was the G&Ts, but Bella could hear Kate laughing out loudly.

'So, Girls, are you coming to the club?' asked John.

'No, we're going to stay here,' said Bella. 'We're too old now for clubbing.'

'Okay. Looks like we will just have to chat you women up some more here,' said Craig.

'You're right, we're all too old for clubbing,' John said, smiling with a cheeky grin.

It was now close to 2am, and the lights were coming on in the bar. The bouncers began prodding the last customers to finish their drinks and get going. The group all knocked back their drinks and headed for the takeaway. Bella got ravenous after a few drinks, and it was a ritual now to go for curry cheese chips after the bar.

'Bella, can I have your number?' said John. Bella quickly changed the subject, and John asked again, so she finally entered her number on his phone. Even though Bella had a few drinks on her at this stage, she was still really shy and reserved when it came to men. She felt like she had been born in the wrong era; she was really old fashioned. She still wanted a man to open doors for her and to protect her. She found though these days it was becoming more difficult to meet a gentleman.

Bella often laughed to herself when she would be walking into a bar as she would find herself holding the door open for the men. Or in a tight, crowded bar she would let them pass by first. If she didn't, they would mow her down to get past. Bella thought she had seen it all until the night a man had been running through the crowd in the bar to get to the restroom. He didn't make it in time and managed to puke on her as he passed. She could never bring herself to wear those gold sandals again.

Bella was not into one-night stands, and she felt like she didn't fit in. She never felt comfortable the morning after; she had too much respect for herself. Bella was also not willing to settle, just to have a man by her side. Now at 32 with only having had a couple of boyfriends over the years, Bella had grown very independent. She would often say to her friends that if a man doesn't add anything to my life and make me happy, then I will pass.

Bella felt like life could be difficult enough without living with the wrong man. She could also be very opinionated at times and she felt some men were intimidated by her. She always had her guard up, trying to protect herself from meeting the next player who might hurt her. Bella was finding it difficult to distinguish the nice men from all these players she was bumping into. She couldn't understand why she was attracting all these players into her life. She seemed to be like a magnet drawing them in. Bella was still waiting for her fairy-tale ending.

It was Tuesday morning after the bank holiday, and Bella was back at work. She still hadn't heard from John. She was disappointed as she had liked him. She poured herself a cup of hot water and was just squeezing a lemon into it when Emma entered the office kitchen. Joan had always started her day with a glass of hot water and lemon. She used to say it was great for cleansing the system. Bella was going to start the cleanse now, after binge drinking all weekend.

'No coffee, this morning?' asked Emma with surprise.

'No, I'm changing my habits,' explained Bella. 'I don't want to get too predictable.' Bella filled Emma in on her night out.

'Sure, he'll probably text you during the week,' said Emma. 'It's only Tuesday.'

'I doubt it,' said Bella with a sigh. 'Anyway, enough about me. How was your weekend?'

'It was okay. I was busy doing wedding things as usual. I have ordered the wedding cake now and the flowers for the church. On Saturday we spent the day shopping, and it was most productive as my sister got her bridesmaid dress. It's gorgeous; it fits her perfectly. She is lucky she has an amazing figure just like you, Bella. You both would look well in a bin bag.'

'Fantastic, what colour is the dress and the style?' asked Bella.

'A dark red; a long dress with a lace bodice,' said Emma.

'It sounds gorgeous. It will be so nice for a Christmas wedding,' said Bella.

They grabbed their drinks and headed back to their desks. Bella felt the day drag by and at five o'clock, she went to the locker room to get her runners. She met Emma outside in the office car park, and they began their 40-minute walk. It had become a habit now, made even more enjoyable by the lovely warm evening.

'Wait up, Bella; you're walking too fast. I am dying back here!'

'Come on, Emma. You know I hate walking slowly,' said Bella. 'It's good for you! Move it, Emma. You'll thank me when you are looking stunning in your wedding dress.'

Emma was sweating now and red-faced. 'It's like boot camp,' gasped Emma.

The weeks flew by, and now that summer was in full swing, Bella and Kate hit the town most weekends. Not that either of them needed an excuse. They had great fun, but unfortunately, there was no sign of their Prince Charmings. Lately all Bella seemed to be meeting were frogs. She was in her parents' garden one evening, playing fetch with the dog, when she let out a scream—a frog had jumped on her leg.

'What's wrong, Bella?' asked her mum running out into the garden.

'Sorry, mum,' said Bella, 'it was just a frog; I keep meeting them.'

'Really, you don't see many frogs around here,' observed her mum.

'I do,' said Bella.

Her mum finally got the joke and laughed.

'One day, Bella, you will meet your prince, I know it.'

Joan used to say this to Bella too.

It was Sunday lunchtime when Bella woke up with a throbbing head from the night before. She slowly opened her eyes; they felt stiff from the mascara she had left on. She looked down and saw she was still wearing her black cocktail dress. She knew it was going to be a bad day; she felt so sick. She was annoyed at herself for drinking so much. *Why did I drink all those tequila shots the girls were buying me for my birthday?* she thought. Bella really suffered badly with hangovers, and now at 33 she still had not learned. She jumped out of bed and ran to the toilet bowl and puked her guts up.

There was a knock on the bathroom door. Kate shouted in, 'Are you okay, Bella?'

'No, I think I might die.'

'I know, I feel so bad too,' said Kate. 'You want anything in the shop? I am going to have to get a bacon roll to cure me.'

'No, I can't eat. My stomach is in bits,' said Bella. 'Can you bring me a glass of water and two painkillers, please?'

Bella slowly got up off the bathroom floor and snuggled back under her duvet again.

'Here you go, Bella. Take these painkillers, and you will feel better,' said Kate.

'I hope they work. I feel so miserable,' said Bella.

'It was such a good night though,' said Kate.

'Yes, from what I remember of it,' mumbled Bella.

'Do you remember that fit guy you were talking to in the takeaway?' asked Kate.

'Vaguely,' said Bella.

'He seemed very interested in you, and he was just adorable,' said Kate. 'But you didn't give him a chance. I had to run out the door after you!'

'I don't really remember much of my conversation with him, to be honest,' said Bella. 'My feet were hurting from all the dancing, and I just wanted to go home.'

'I'll leave you to recover,' said Kate. 'We can rehash the night later.'

Whenever Bella was feeling unloved and frustrated with still being single, she had a habit of getting drunk to try and release her pain. Alcohol helped her relax and it numbed her so she could escape for a while from her current circumstances. She liked this feeling as she had a habit of overthinking every situation. She found it difficult to switch her thoughts off. However, getting drunk never solved Bella's problems and she just felt miserable after with the hangover. She would then lose any motivation to do anything about her circumstances. She would continue to complain to herself about life being cruel and unfair and would wallow in self-pity.

Bella awoke to the noise of her phone vibrating on her bedside table and looked at who was calling: MUM. She counted slowly to three and then answered in a bubbly voice, 'Hi, Mum, how are you?'

'I'm just ringing to see if you are coming out for the roast,' her mum said. 'It's getting late.'

Over the years the Sunday roast was a ritual in the O'Sullivan house. This shared family time around the kitchen table was rarely missed without a good reason. Good and bad news was all shared over the roast. It seemed to be the place where the family all opened up to each other. Sometimes this resulted in a few disagreements but mostly it was a table filled with love and support for each other.

'Sorry, Mum, I forgot to tell you my friends are taking me out for dinner this evening for my birthday; we are going to the new Italian.' Bella hated lying to her mum, but she couldn't tell her she could barely lift her head from the pillow. Talking was actually painful for Bella and thinking of eating roast beef made her want to throw up again. She couldn't bear the thought of listening to a lecture from her mum about drinking too much.

Bella spent the day in bed. All she could keep down was water. She knew Joan would never approve of her behaviour as she had been such an early riser, getting up at 6am every day of the week without fail.

It was mid-week before Bella had fully recovered from her hangover. The hangovers seemed to be getting worse as she got older. Bella knew she needed to change her behaviour as this binge drinking every weekend was now affecting her physical and mental health.

Joan regularly reminded Bella of the importance of a healthy body and mind.

Bella remembered always being the last one still sitting at the dinner table in Joan's house as a kid. 'You need to eat your greens, Bella. They're good for you,' Joan would remind her, proceeding to mash the cabbage into her potatoes. Bella hated vegetables and once she even tried putting vinegar on cauliflower to take away the taste and ensure that she didn't miss out on Joan's homemade dessert.

Joan herself had always been very healthy, and up to her 70th year, she had never spent a single night in the hospital. One day though, while Joan was dressing, she discovered a lump on her breast. Two weeks later she had a mastectomy. This was the first time Bella had seen Joan so upset and worried. It passed though, as Joan did not let her recovery from surgery control her.

Bella's mum helped to nurse Joan back to health, and she would give her a daily Guinness to build her up. Joan drank it even though she never usually drank alcohol; well, apart from the odd glass of champagne. Joan accepted her health, and she made peace with her new body. Her positive attitude had helped her to recover from her surgery quickly. Joan was grateful for every day she woke up breathing. Joan and her husband Martin were soon out dancing again. They had met at a dance, and they had continued to waltz and jive whenever there was music. Their dancing kept them fit. Their house continually had country music playing and often Bella would catch them dancing around their sitting room.

Joan had taught Bella how to dance. Bella often thought that if she did get married she'd be able to skip the dance classes.

Bella's entries in her journal

Three things I am grateful for

O'Connor's Bar

Shoes

Country music

Joan's wise words to me

Celebrate the little wins in life as they will keep you motivated and increase your confidence.

Write down your negative thoughts and burn them. Replace them with positive ones.

One day you will meet your prince. I know it.

Drink hot water and lemon for the cleanse.

Eat your greens; they are good for you.

Someone I need to send love to

I send love to John for not contacting me.

Positive affirmation

I am so happy and grateful now that I love myself and I take responsibility for my own happy life.

CHAPTER 3

A soul never dies

Bella's day at work could not go fast enough. After work, she had planned to visit her friend Annie who'd recently had a baby. As Bella was driving to Annie's house, she felt the excitement building up at thoughts of seeing baby Charlie and, of course, Annie's new house.

Bella loved driving through the countryside. It was a beautiful sunny evening, and as she drove by the neighbouring houses, she could see children out playing in their gardens, people mowing their lawns, and people walking their dogs. Everyone just seemed to be so happy, out enjoying the sun. *Thank God, for technology, I definitely would have got lost without it, with my poor sense of direction. All these narrow winding country roads.*

Bella pulled into Annie's driveway. The charming four-bed cottage was surrounded by a lovely stone wall. The beautiful blossom trees and the array of colourful flowers in the window boxes caught Bella's eye immediately. Bella thought the cottage looked so pretty—it was like something from a painting. *Annie is one lucky lady*, Bella thought as she gave a little knock on the door, afraid of waking Charlie. Annie opened the door smiling and gave her a big hug.

'Hi, Annie. Your house is fabulous. Is Charlie asleep? I am dying to see him.'

'No, he just woke up now, looking for his next bottle. Come on into the sitting room. I want to hear all the news,' continued Annie. 'It's been so long.'

'Sure, but I have no news,' said Bella.

'How's the love life?' asked Annie, looking for a story.

'Well, it's non-existent,' mused Bella, 'but a girl can dream and live in hope.'

'Bella, there is always some man chasing you. I think you are just too fussy. I will let you in on a secret, Bella: no man will ever be perfect.'

'I know,' acknowledged Bella. 'I am not looking for *perfect*. All I want is a man who respects me and is kind to me. Anyhow, enough about me.' Bella handed Annie a blue gift bag, a bottle of champagne and a picture frame she had wrapped in silver paper.

'It's just something small', said Bella, 'for Charlie and the new house.'

Annie opened the gift bag and lifted out a white shirt, blue cord trousers, and a red cardigan. 'Oh, this outfit is so cute!' She unwrapped the crystal picture frame and exclaimed, 'Oh, that's fabulous too. I love it. Thank you, Bella. I have a lovely family picture from Charlie's christening that will be perfect for it.'

James came in, holding Charlie and feeding him a bottle.

'Congrats, James,' said Bella as she jumped up from the couch and walked over to Charlie for a closer look.

'It's good to see you, Bella,' said James.

'Oh, Charlie is just adorable,' Bella said excitedly.

'Can I hold him after his bottle, James?' Bella asked, smiling at Annie.

'Sure,' said James. 'It will be good practice for you, for when you have your own someday.'

'Is he good at night, Annie?' asked Bella.

'Not too bad! I got about four hours sleep last night,' Annie said, smiling back.

'Four hours!' Bella exclaimed. 'God, I would die without my sleep. How do you cope? Are you not wrecked?'

'You just get used to it, Bella. You really have no choice. And, he's worth all the sleepless nights,' said Annie yawning, looking lovingly at her little darling. 'Come on, while Charlie's being fed. I will give you the grand tour of the house.'

Bella jumped up eagerly and accompanied Annie into the kitchen.

'Oh wow! I love your kitchen. It just feels so welcoming, it has such character about it.' Bella looked over to the old wooden corner dresser filled with a collection of china teacups and saucers.

'The dresser is really pretty too!' exclaimed Bella.

'Do you like the colour?' asked Annie. 'James painted it. My grandma loved that dresser, and we could not bring ourselves to throw it out, plus we needed somewhere for all her china. It's a family heirloom now.'

'I do. The duck-egg blue is fabulous,' said Bella. 'It goes really well with the window blinds.'

'We are just so lucky my grandma left me her cottage,' said Annie. 'If she hadn't, we probably would still be stuck renting somewhere. House prices have really increased with the lack of supply.'

'It has all worked out for you,' Bella said, smiling at Annie.

Annie loved to cook and she had a lovely bright kitchen to cook in. It felt so homey to Bella. There was a lovely scent of baking and it reminded Bella of Joan's kitchen. 'What, you cooked scones as well?' Bella asked, amazed.

'Yes, I did, especially for you,' Annie said with a smile in her voice.

'You are superwoman!' said Bella. 'How did you find the time?'

'There is always time, Bella, for what you love doing and James was off work today to give me a hand.'

Bella had shared a house with Annie while they were in college. Annie had loved baking then, regularly trying out new recipes. Bella was her willing food critic who was not too hard to please as she just loved anything sweet. Annie's scones were truly amazing, and in their college days they both used to put a big blob of clotted cream and jam on them. Not very healthy, but it made them taste so good.

As they walked around the rest of the house, Bella could see that it glowed with love, warmth and new parenthood. Once the entire house had been inspected, they headed back to the kitchen for scones and two pots of tea.

'This china makes me feel very posh indeed,' said Bella.

'I don't miss the chipped mugs we used to have in the house; or trying to find a clean mug,' said Annie laughing.

'I really don't know how we lived in that house,' said Bella. 'It was so cold and mouldy.'

'I couldn't live like that now,' said Annie. 'I'm too old and I like my comfort too much.'

'I suppose back then we were not around the house much. We were usually out partying somewhere,' reminisced Bella.

'We did have such fun,' agreed Annie. 'I miss our college days. Now, back to reality,' she said, handing Charlie to Bella.

'He is so tiny, Annie,' Bella exclaimed as she cradled Charlie. Ten minutes later, he was snuggled into her, asleep. 'He looks so peaceful,' said Bella looking up at the clock. 'God, I'd better go, Annie, it's nearly midnight! I am getting carried away here.'

Bella got up from the couch, passing over Charlie and lifting her handbag.

'It was lovely to see you, Bella. I really enjoyed the catch-up. You have to come again soon,' Annie stressed in an insistent tone.

'I most certainly will,' said Bella, heading toward the door. 'Night, night.'

When Bella arrived back at her apartment it felt so cold, empty and dark. Kate was away with work and Bella was missing her company. Bella had really enjoyed the visit with Annie, but for some reason now, lying in her bed, she felt a wave of despair. She was happy for Annie, seeing how content she was to be living in the cottage with James and Charlie. But Bella couldn't help but wonder when she would be content like that. When would she get married and have a house and a baby? She suddenly felt alone and unloved.

As a teenager, Bella had imagined herself being married by 30, having at least two kids and living in a home filled with love and joy. She had the family picture perfectly set out in her head. The apartment she was currently living in did not fit in with this picture. She was questioning now where she had gone so wrong. She felt like life was passing her by too quickly. Everyone except Bella seemed to be moving on in life with their partners and family. She felt stuck and frustrated. She grabbed her journal and even though she felt disconnected from gratitude, she began to write.

> *Why me, God? Why am I here all alone? What is your plan for me? I don't think the nuns will have me. I don't understand why I am still single. Where is my soulmate? What meaning has my life? Please help me, God. All I want is to be loved and be happy.*

The page was now wet from her tears, but Bella felt so relieved getting all her questions down on paper. All she needed now were the answers or someone to talk some sense into her.

'Joan, where are you when I need you?' she said to herself, even though Bella knew quite well what advice Joan would give her. In her mind, she heard Joan's soothing voice consoling her. *Bella, don't worry about meeting the love of your life. Be patient. It will happen. Have faith and believe and then he will appear in your life. Enjoy life's journey and see everything that happens in your life as an opportunity to learn and grow. Always remember: your challenges can be your greatest blessings.*

Joan herself had not married Martin until she was 35. This did give Bella some hope.

It was one year now since Joan had passed away at the age of 89. It had been a tough year for Bella and she was still grieving for her friend deeply. Joan had been there for her, for every celebration—birthdays, communion, confirmation and graduation. Joan was also there for the hard times too, like when Bella's uncle Liam had died suddenly, when men broke her heart or when something or someone had upset her. Joan always had the words to comfort and console Bella and somehow she would make everything in the world okay again.

Bella recalled going into the hospital to visit Joan the day before she died. When Bella entered the room, she could see Martin sitting at Joan's bedside, looking tearful and holding his wife's hand. Bella had visited Joan every evening after work for the previous three weeks, but something was different about today. When Bella first saw Joan lying in the hospital bed that day, she got a shock, as Joan just looked so frail and weak. *Old age is really cruel,* thought Bella. Joan was unable to speak, but when she saw Bella, her eyes lit up, and she started to smile. Bella smiled back at Joan.

'I am going for a coffee, Bella,' Martin said. 'I will leave you both for a few minutes. I will give your mum a call, Bella, and update her. It might be best if Elaine and Alan, your sister and brother, come in soon.' Bella thought Martin looked so tired; he had lost the sparkle in his eyes.

Bella's parents had flown to the UK the week before to see their daughter Una who was graduating from college as a physiotherapist. They were not due back until the following day, and Bella really felt their absence.

She froze in disbelief, for Martin was warning her about the imminence of Joan's death. Bella couldn't get any words out even though she had so much to say to Joan. Bella noticed tears had started to roll down Joan's face too. Bella was trying to stay strong as she did not want Joan to see her getting upset. She tried to comfort Joan, but her heart was breaking. Bella knew this was going to be the last time she would see her dear friend. Bella couldn't handle it. Joan was forever the strong one comforting Bella, and she was so good at it.

'Joan, I am sorry, but I have to go now,' Bella said. 'I will see you later,' and she softly kissed her cheek. 'I will love you forever.'

Bella couldn't leave the hospital fast enough; she just couldn't cope with what was happening. She drove back to her apartment and sobbed uncontrollably. That night Bella got a call from her sister Elaine saying that Joan had passed away peacefully.

After Joan's death, Bella had felt guilty and ashamed for how she had left the hospital that evening, so abruptly.

On the day of Joan's funeral as Bella was walking behind Joan's coffin to the graveyard, through her tears, she had spotted a single white feather lying in the grass. She knew it was sent to comfort her. She remembered Joan used to love seeing white feathers, and whenever she did, she would say to Bella an angel is near. Joan had been very spiritual and she had a special painting of a single white feather in her sitting room.

Every day after Joan passed, Bella visited Martin, bringing him a dinner her mum had cooked for him. The house was not the same, without Joan there. All her belongings were there, but the life was gone from the house. It felt empty. Bella missed the smell of baking, the music, but most of all, she missed her dear friend Joan. Martin had said to Bella that he did not know how to live without his wife. It was painful for Bella to see Martin looking so lost.

Martin died six months later in his sleep, heartbroken.

Bella was devastated, losing them both, and to console herself she thought of Joan's words to her in the past: 'Remember, Bella, when I am gone: A soul never dies.'

Bella's entries in her journal

Three things I am grateful for

Flowers

Scones with clotted cream and jam

White feathers

Joan's wise words to me

Don't worry about meeting the love of your life. Be patient. Have faith and believe.

Enjoy life's journey and see everything that happens in your life as an opportunity to learn and grow.

Your challenges can be your greatest blessings.

Whenever you see a white feather, an angel is near.

Remember, Bella: a soul never dies.

Someone I need to send love to

I send love to myself for my negative thoughts.

Positive affirmation

I am so happy and grateful I am loved. I have inner peace and think positive thoughts. I face every problem with a smile.

CHAPTER 4

A burning desire

As the months passed by Bella realised she would have to learn how to control her mind. All these negative thoughts of feeling unloved were only making her feel worse. She was not seeing the blessings she had in her life and was only focused on what was missing. Bella knew she had to change what was going on inside her before she could change any circumstance in her outside world.

She realised that she was solely going to be responsible for changing her life. She decided to let go of this family image she'd had for a while and to trust in the universe. The pressure of trying to meet a man, find a home and have kids was making her feel overwhelmed, anxious and fearful. Her happiness in life had become dependent upon this dream.

She replaced the family image with an image of herself smiling and standing outside her own home. Bella knew she had to fall in love with herself first before any man ever would. She was reminded of Joan's words to her: 'Bella, the most important relationship you will have in this life is with yourself.'

The first step she took was to embrace her single life and she started to focus on her unique characteristics and strengths. She knew that she was a very determined person, and knew that if she made a promise to herself, she would keep it.

When she had finally quietened her mind and reflected on what she really wanted in life, she discovered she had a burning desire to purchase a house.

Bella at 33 then decided to set herself a goal: *I will purchase a house before I turn 40.* When she thought about turning 40, she felt anxious, afraid of having nothing significant in her life. She knew if she purchased a house by 40 it would make her happy. She was sick of renting, and there was no security in it. She had lost count of the times she'd had to move out unexpectedly when the landlord notified her they were selling the house or the apartment. Bella wanted to enjoy the benefits of homeownership. She wanted to choose her own furniture, hang up pictures. She was at an age now where she longed for more space. She hated having to keep all her personal effects in her bedroom. She wanted to be in control of her home rather than being reliant on the landlord to fix any problems.

Bella realised that prior to this, without a goal, she had been plodding along in life, just waiting. Waiting for something to happen, waiting to meet a man, and most importantly waiting to be happy. She needed to get out of her comfort zone now, take action and make things happen for herself.

Bella wondered if this was where she had been going wrong in the past as she had never set personal goals for anything, be it her career, health, finances, or relationships. Bella had been leaving everything to chance and luck and waiting for things to happen, instead of creating and manifesting what she wanted in her own life.

If she was going to achieve her goal of purchasing a house, Bella knew she would have to conquer her self-doubt. To purchase a house by herself, she would also have to start saving, as houses in Ireland were so expensive. Bella was earning an average salary, and now she was even more determined to get a bonus at work.

Bella had been an average student in school, but she'd had no idea what she wanted to do when she finished school as nothing had stood out to her. She could tell everyone what she didn't want to do though—she didn't want to be a nurse as even the sight of blood made her feel weak. She still has nightmares following the week she spent working at a nursing home. She knew she was not cut out for caring for people. Bella figured a business degree would be a safe bet as she could always get a job in an office. So she enrolled and completed a business degree that she really enjoyed. This had led her into her current sales role.

Bella felt tired at work, from having made such important life decisions. She started to yawn at her desk when Emma came back from a customer meeting.

'How is your day going, Bella?' she asked with a smile.

'Grand. Sorry. I am really tired today,' said Bella.

'At least Ruth is off on vacation for the next two weeks,' Emma said teasingly.

'I know!' Bella exclaimed. 'Peace for a few weeks, at least! Having said that, she's been really nice and supportive to me lately. I was shocked when she praised me at the team meeting last week for exceeding my sales target for September.'

Emma shook her head in amazement. 'Hmm! Any plans for the weekend, Bella?'

'No, I'm staying quiet this weekend,' Bella replied, shaking her head.

'Really? But why? You are not heading out?' Emma asked, surprised.

Bella thought for a moment and then said, 'I have to stay in some weekends.' She paused briefly and then tried to explain her actions further to Emma. 'Well, I'm holding off on partying until your hen; it's only three weeks away.' The excitement in Bella's voice was palpable.

'I don't recognise you, Bella! You are getting too sensible,' remarked Emma.

'Are there many attending your hen?' Bella inquired.

'About 20,' replied Emma. 'The bus is all booked.'

'That's awesome,' said Bella. 'We can all get the bus up and down to Dublin. It will save us driving for two hours there and back, especially when we are hung-over coming back.'

Just then, the phone started to ring. This was the call for them both to get back to work. Bella and Emma were busy for the rest of the day on sales calls. The weeks flew by and Bella continued making progress at work and dreaming of her house.

It was Sunday morning after Emma's hen party. Bella woke up late and looked around her hotel room for her bottled water. Her throat was dry and she felt so thirsty. Her feet ached. She immediately felt glad she had booked Monday off work to recover from all the partying. The hen party had been *mental*. They went to a posh restaurant for dinner, followed by cocktails and dancing at the nightclub.

Bella had bumped into her ex-boyfriend Keith in the nightclub. He was looking as handsome as ever. They had dated previously for a while, but Keith was not interested in her or in making a commitment. He was only looking for a casual relationship to pass the time. Bella had thought she would be able to change Keith's mind about this, and he would fall madly in love with her once he got to know her. This didn't happen, so she ended the relationship when she finally listened to her intuition. Joan had always said to her, 'Your intuition is your greatest gift. It will guide you right in life.'

Bella knew in her heart that she wanted a committed, meaningful relationship in her life, and Keith was not able to give her this. Keith would text her every so often, but Bella had lost interest.

She was polite when she bumped into Keith at the bar in the nightclub. After a few pleasantries, she left and joined Emma on the dance floor. Her favourite song was playing. She was proud of herself for walking away from Keith. At this point in her life, she had too much respect for herself to settle for anything less than what she truly deserved. She really wanted more than ever though to meet her prince.

Back at her apartment, while unpacking her pink suitcase, Bella looked over to a black-and-white photo on her bedroom windowsill. The photo was in a pretty white frame in the shape of a butterfly. She loved that photo. Joan and Martin looked so happy on their wedding day. Bella saw them as the perfect couple. They had such love for each other; it was indescribable. She thought to herself how fortunate they were to have met each other. In Bella's eyes, they were the epitome of what true soulmates should be.

Bella had such a close relationship with Joan; her older friend was like a grandmother to her. Sadly, Bella had never met either of her grandmothers as they had both passed away quite young before Bella was born, so this relationship was missing from her life. Joan filled this void. Joan and Martin had no kids of their own. They had spent years trying, and after several miscarriages, they had accepted that parenthood was just not meant to be for them. Martin had planted several rose bushes in their garden in remembrance. There was a wooden bench beside the rose bushes, and Joan and Martin would spend hours there, just sitting in the garden together.

Joan and Martin had become treasured family friends to the O'Sullivans.

As a kid, Bella and her siblings would go to Joan's house after school. Bella loved Friday evenings in particular at Joan's house. They would all sit together and watch black-and-white films on Joan's small TV. They were all so happy drinking hot cocoa and eating cake, it was magical.

Joan had taught Bella how to bake. Bella used to love baking with Joan, and she and her siblings would all dip their fingers in the bowl of whatever Joan would be baking at that time. Joan never followed a recipe book, but somehow she would make the most delicious sponges, scones, tarts and shortbread. Bella remembered her kitchen always smelled so good, just like the inside of a bakery. Even with all this baking, Joan had a fantastic figure, and she enjoyed a serving of dessert every day.

Bella loved Joan's guidance in her life. She remembered back to her first interview after college when she was living with her parents. Joan had come into the kitchen.

'Morning, Bella,' Joan had said with a smile. 'Just popped in to wish you good luck for your interview today.'

'Thanks, Joan,' Bella replied, looking nervous and swirling her cornflakes around the bowl.

'You look so smart in your grey suit, Bella,' Joan observed, looking her over. Joan knew Bella so well, and she could sense how nervous she was.

After some consideration, Joan said in a firm voice, 'Put the kettle on, and let us have a cuppa.'

Joan used to say, no matter what the problem was, it could be solved over a cuppa and a chat. Joan poured the tea, and she started to coach Bella through some possible interview questions.

When the actual interview was over, Bella went straight to Joan's house. Joan was busy in the kitchen icing a sponge when Bella ran in.

'I got it! I got it!' shouted Bella overjoyed and waving her arms in the air.

'Well done, Bella. I am delighted for you,' said Joan, giving her an affectionate hug. 'I just knew you would get the job.'

'How did you know? I certainly didn't.'

'I believe in you, Bella. How could they resist a lovely young woman like yourself? They are so lucky to have you, never underestimate the potential you have. I was in town today and I bought you a new bag to help you look the part,' she said smiling. 'Pop upstairs and get it. It's in my room.'

A few minutes later, Bella came down, modelling the black shoulder bag.

'I love it, Joan. Thank you so much, it's perfect. I see you bought yourself some new clothes too,' Bella said. Joan was thrifty, so Bella was a bit surprised seeing all Joan's new clothes laid out on her bed.

'I did, Bella. I needed to get a few bits for my trip to Canada. You know it's only a few weeks away.' Martin's nephew Sean lived in Canada, and they tried to visit him every year. Sean was married to a Canadian woman, Audrey, and they had a son, Gavin. Bella had got to know Sean's family over the years as they frequently visited Ireland. Gavin was her age and he would always meet up with the O'Sullivans when he was in Ireland. They would all go fishing, horse riding and spend hours lazing on the beach together. The evenings would be spent watching movies in Joan's house.

Bella smiled again at the picture of her beloved couple. She missed Joan so much.

Bella's entries in her journal

Three things I am grateful for

My friendship with Joan

My business degree

Black-and-white films

Joan's wise words to me

The most important relationship you will have in this life is with yourself.

Your intuition is your greatest gift and it will guide you right in life.

No matter what the problem is it can be solved over a cuppa and a chat.

I believe in you.

Never underestimate the potential you have.

Someone I need to send love to

I send love to Keith for not falling in love with me.

Positive affirmation

I am so happy and grateful now that my goal of purchasing a house by 40 has come true.

CHAPTER 5

Taking action

Growing up as a kid in the eighties, Bella did not have much money. Her parents did their best, but Bella was one of four kids. Her mother and father both worked in a local medical device factory, but on their wages, after paying their mortgage, they were just living week by week. Her parents had promoted education to their kids and encouraged them to get a degree so they would not end up struggling in life as they had. Bella often used to wonder how her mother had got married at 19. It just seemed so young to Bella, and she couldn't imagine having a baby at 22 either! Bella did see the benefits of it now, however, as both her parents were still relatively young, in their late fifties. They both still had plenty of energy to run around after their grandkids and they were enjoying being grandparents.

Bella, like her parents, was very generous with her money; she loved helping people as it genuinely made her feel good. Joan had taught her to show kindness to herself and others, and would say, in this world, those who give really do benefit the most in life.

When Bella first started working after college, she used to love having money of her own to buy clothes and shoes. She loved not being dependent on her parents. As a little girl, Bella would complain to her mum frequently when she would have to wear her older sister Elaine's hand-me-downs. While wearing her lovely new outfit, Elaine would be smiling at Bella. Their mother promised Bella that because she did not get a new holy communion or confirmation dress, she would buy Bella her wedding dress. Looking back, Bella often thought that her mother must have known from the start that this was going to be a safe bet, since the moment was so far away. Bella's siblings used to slag her, saying she had second child syndrome.

These days, Bella spent a lot of her income on entertainment, dinners out, night outs, cinema trips and weekends away. Sometimes she would have no money left in her bank account, but if she really wanted to go out, she would go to the ATM and withdraw using her credit card. A typical weekend for her was going out and then suffering the dreaded hangover, making Sundays a complete write-off.

Looking back, Bella was kicking herself for not saving in her twenties and for wasting so much of her money. She felt like she hadn't grown up properly yet as she had no house, she wasn't married, and she had no kids.

Her brother would regularly joke that Bella had been out fishing again all weekend and had caught nothing. She did have fun going out but, on this particular Monday, she knew that things were about to change. It was time to take action on her dreams.

Bella had come up with her seven-year plan of saving for a house deposit. The words *save, save, save*, were now engraved in her mind.

Joan had a habit of saving for what she wanted, and if she didn't have the money, she wouldn't buy it until she had the money to do so. Bella was not familiar with this concept and she would often take out a loan if she wanted to go on a sun holiday instead of saving for it. Bella also loved to use her credit card.

Today, though, Bella would start to take daily steps toward achieving her goal. Taking these small daily steps would be critical so she did not become too overwhelmed with her goal of purchasing a house. Joan used to say that Bella had a habit of overcomplicating things and she needed to keep them simple.

Bella pulled out her credit card from her purse and quickly cut it up. She wondered if she would be able to live without it as she was so dependent on it. She then made herself a goal card by writing on a piece of white cardboard, '*A home for Bella by 40*'. She placed the goal card in her purse where her credit card had been. She needed to be reminded of her goal every time she opened her purse to spend. She had to start becoming conscious of what she was spending her money on and asking herself if she *needed* or just *wanted* the item. Bella went online and paid off her credit card. Then, as she only had a few repayments left on her car loan, she paid that off too.

Bella then took a piece of paper and started to jot down the ways she could potentially save money and reduce her day-to-day spending. Three pages later she had a long list of cutbacks she needed to make. She logged onto her banking app and reviewed her spending for the last six months. She was amazed and quite shocked at how much she was actually spending on nights out, dinners, clothes and, of course, shoes.

Bella needed to understand the steps involved in purchasing a house, and she was now willing to invest the time in her personal growth. She signed up for a free housing seminar for first-time buyers hosted by her bank. The seminar was held in a local hotel. She attended it by herself and noticed it was full of couples.

She had so many questions on purchasing a house, the conveyance process and applying for a mortgage. The seminar was very informative, and she left with a step-by-step information pack on purchasing a house. On driving home from the seminar, she realised she needed to show the bank she would be able to manage the monthly mortgage payments by herself. The bank needed to have confidence in Bella's ability to repay a mortgage. She needed to show them she was financially stable.

An idea popped into her head: *Get an apartment by yourself. You can afford it on your salary if you make some cutbacks.* As rents were so high, the cost of renting an apartment by herself would be the same cost as having a mortgage. The bank would then be able to see she could afford a mortgage by herself.

Bella could now see how important her career was going to be in helping her to become financially stable. In her twenties, she loved working as a receptionist for a large multinational. She thought a job as a receptionist would be a good opportunity for her to gain experience of working in an office environment. It would help her develop a good understanding of what each of the departments were responsible for.

As a receptionist she got to know everyone in the office and spoke with everyone from the lowest to the highest tier. Everyone was always so nice to the receptionist. It really helped to improve her confidence, and she became much more social. As a child, Bella was very shy, and at birthday parties or any crowded events, she would find herself going over to Joan and sitting on her lap.

While working at reception, Bella soon developed an interest in the sales department. She used to watch Nora, the vice president of sales, come into the office. Nora had such an air of confidence about her whenever she walked into the room. Bella used to admire all her clothes and shoes and considered her trendy. Nora's team loved working with her as she was a strong leader they all admired and trusted. Nora was able to motivate her team toward success.

Every morning when Nora walked into the office, Bella used to sit there and imagine having her job. Bella would visualise herself coming into the office being the vice president of sales, and it excited her.

A year at reception passed by quickly for Bella, and one day out of the blue, a great opportunity came to her. This opportunity was going to change Bella's career. Nora had come to the reception area, talking rapidly on her phone, looking a bit more stressed than usual.

Something's up with Nora today, Bella thought. Nora was usually so calm and bubbly.

'It's okay, Niamh, don't worry,' Nora said in a sympathetic voice. 'Just take care of yourself.' She then hung up the phone and looked over at Bella sitting behind the reception desk.

'Morning, Nora, how are you today?' Bella asked with a smile.

'Not good,' Nora answered in a distressed voice. 'I have important customer meetings all day and Niamh has just phoned to inform me that she fell and broke her arm last night. She needs surgery and will be out for a few weeks. How am I going to make things work without her?' said Nora.

'Poor Niamh! What will you do?' Bella said in sympathy.

Nora thought it over for a bit and then said, 'I will have to call the agency and see if they can send over a temp to cover Niamh. I doubt though I will get someone today at such short notice.'

'I have an idea,' Bella said quietly. 'I might be able to help. I could be your PA for the day. I was to give Kara her final training on reception today but Kara can easily cover the reception desk by herself, while I help you out.'

Nora's eyes had started to shine. 'You are a star, Bella! That would be such a great help.'

Bella suddenly felt quite nervous and panicky. Why had she suggested this to Nora? What was she thinking? Negative thoughts started to fill her mind. Her inner critic pestered at her: *What do you know about being a PA, Bella? Do you know anything about sales?*

It was all negative.

'Why don't you come to my office in ten minutes?' Nora got straight down to business. 'I need to brief you ahead of the customer meetings.'

'Okay,' Bella said, 'I'll bring you a coffee too. You look like you need it.'

Bella really enjoyed her day working as Nora's PA. Nora was also impressed with Bella's performance. She asked if Bella could stay in the role until Niamh was fit to return to work. Bella was thrilled—she would be getting more experience in sales and for the opportunity to work with Nora who was just so inspiring.

On Bella's last day working as a PA, Nora asked her to call into her office. Bella knocked on the office door.

'Come in,' Nora said. She got up from her chair and handed Bella a big bouquet of flowers and a large box of chocolates. 'I just wanted to say a special thank you, Bella, for covering while Niamh was on leave. You were wonderful and a pleasure to work with. You had everything organised and managed so well for me.'

Bella blushed. She was so thankful for the positive feedback. She had learned from Joan that whatever job you are doing in life, you should always give it your best effort. This had certainly paid off for Bella.

'Have you ever thought of a career in sales?' Nora asked Bella in a warm voice.

Bella was a bit shocked at the question but quickly said yes. She left out the part though where she had visualised herself as Nora working as the VP of sales. With a dazzling smile, Bella remarked, 'I really enjoyed working in the sales department. It was such an interesting experience.'

'I have been watching you perform,' Nora explained. 'And I really do think you would be excellent in sales.'

With surprise, Bella said, 'You do? Don't you think I am a bit quiet and shy for a sales position?'

'No,' Nora said. 'You only *think* that about yourself, and there is no harm in those qualities. It's your attitude that matters most, Bella. If you are passionate about something you will be good at it as you will enjoy it. It will become natural to you and you will gain more confidence with experience. You are young, Bella, and have plenty of time to learn. I too was shy, and look at me now—you would never think it. Sometimes you just need to step out of your comfort zone to succeed.'

Nora reminded Bella of Joan's words, 'The only way to grow in life is to step out of your comfort zone.'

'Thanks for the encouragement, Nora,' said Bella.

'There is a junior sales position coming up. I think you should apply. You would be perfect for the role,' Nora continued. She handed Bella the job specification paperwork.

Bella had an interview the following week. She had been delighted when Nora came in one morning and offered her the sales role.

Bella worked with Nora for almost eight years. She was crushed when Nora handed in her notice. Nora had decided to move to the USA with her husband and kids. Ruth Fahy, an external candidate, replaced Nora.

Bella's entries in her journal

Three things I am grateful for

Nora

The opportunity to work in sales

My salary

Joan's wise words to me

In this world, those who give really do benefit the most in life.

Show kindness to yourself and others.

Don't overcomplicate things, keep them simple.

Give every job your best effort.

The only way to grow in life is to step out of your comfort zone.

Someone I need to send love to

I send love to Nora for leaving.

Positive affirmation

I am so happy and grateful I trust and believe in myself. I attract what I need and I am successful.

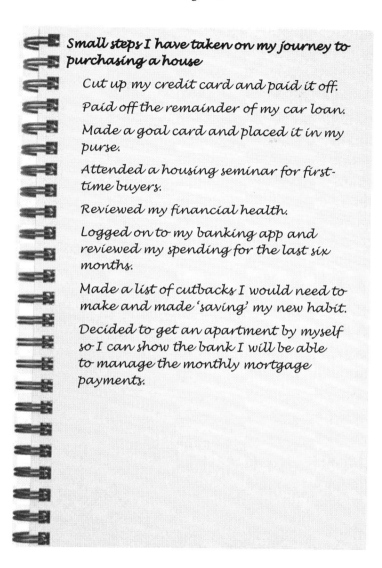

Small steps I have taken on my journey to purchasing a house

Cut up my credit card and paid it off.

Paid off the remainder of my car loan.

Made a goal card and placed it in my purse.

Attended a housing seminar for first-time buyers.

Reviewed my financial health.

Logged on to my banking app and reviewed my spending for the last six months.

Made a list of cutbacks I would need to make and made 'saving' my new habit.

Decided to get an apartment by myself so I can show the bank I will be able to manage the monthly mortgage payments.

CHAPTER 6

Looking for the positives

So far in life, Bella had never had the experience of living by herself. If she ever did achieve her goal of purchasing a house, it would mean living alone as she was single. She played around with the idea of possibly renting out rooms when she purchased her house, but she really could not see herself renting to strangers. All her friends except Kate were now living with their partners.

Bella could imagine herself getting protective of her own house. When she started to picture housemates spilling wine on her carpet, marking the walls, or breaking something in her house, she knew it would not work. All this would not bother Bella if she was renting, but it would be a different story if it were her own house.

She decided she would need to set a test for herself to see if she could actually survive living alone. The thought did scare her, and she wondered how she would cope living by herself and whether she would feel isolated.

Bella was driving home from the supermarket and was so deep in thought that she missed the street to her apartment. How was she going to tell Kate that she had decided to move out of the apartment? Bella would need to give Kate one month's notice, and she would also need to find an affordable apartment.

The day came when Bella was ready to tell Kate she had decided to move out. Bella was cooking her signature lasagne when Kate returned from work. Bella smiled at her friend and asked how work was. 'Busy,' said Kate. 'I'm wrecked. My head is fried from spreadsheets all day, and I have double the work now since my manager is on leave.'

Bella wondered if this particular evening was the right time to tell Kate.

Bella put the spatula down and asked, 'You want some lasagne? I've got loads here.'

Kate sighed with contentment. 'Yes, please. It will save me cooking. You are the best.'

After dinner, Bella went to the freezer and pulled out the ice-cream. Hot chocolate brownies and ice-cream were definitely going to be needed.

'Wow,' said Kate, 'Dessert too!'

'I need to soften you up,' Bella said nervously.

'This sounds worrying,' said Kate. 'What have I done? Sorry, I did eat some of your cookies, Bella. And I did borrow your red handbag, and I know the apartment is a bit messy, and it's my turn to clean.'

'You are okay, Kate,' said Bella laughing. 'It's not any of that! I've been thinking about my life lately,' said Bella.

'I know this is deep,' she continued, 'but I just feel stuck. I think it's time I take control of my own life and start to save for a house.'

'That's an amazing plan,' said Kate.

Bella continued, 'It's just that I think I need to move out now to see if I can live by myself.'

'Move out!' Kate exclaimed looking gutted. 'Do you not like living with me? Can you not stay renting here and save too?'

'I love living with you,' Bella said emphatically, 'and you know I do. I will really miss living with you, but I need to do this for myself. I need to see how I get on renting an apartment by myself and show the bank I can afford to pay a mortgage by myself.

'I've been waiting too long for the perfect man to show up in my life to change my circumstance, but what happens if I don't ever meet this man, Kate? Not everyone ends up getting married in life.'

This was a difficult conversation for Bella to have with her friend. They were both single and she didn't want to make Kate feel bad.

'Bella, we're only 33; we have loads of time yet.'

'Do we really?' said Bella. 'I worked it out, and it's going to take me years to save for a deposit by myself. I need to start taking action now. I don't want to get stuck in the rent trap. I want to own my own home and invest in my future. If I really don't like living by myself, I'll either have to make more of an effort on the dating scene—I may even join Tinder—or I'll have to get comfortable with renting with strangers.' Bella could be very black and white at times.

They ate their dessert and Kate was very quiet and later disappeared to her room for the evening. Kate needed to get her head around the idea as she would miss Bella. With her plans, Bella had now turned Kate's world upside down too. While Bella was relieved that she had been honest with Kate, she still didn't feel good. Yet there was no going back now on her decision as the wheels were in motion and she was moving out.

It was Saturday evening. A month had passed since Bella announced she was moving out. Sarah, Amy and Laura had called over to the apartment for Bella's farewell dinner.

The doorbell rang. 'I will get it,' said Bella, 'I think it's the pizza.' A minute later, Bella came into the kitchen with two large pepperoni pizzas. 'Dig in, girls,' said Bella. Kate poured them all wine.

'I just can't believe you are moving out,' said Amy. 'We will miss calling over for these dinners.'

'Sure, you still can call,' said Bella. 'You will just have two apartments to visit now.' The girls could not understand why Bella was moving out. She on the other hand was getting excited about moving out and starting her new journey of living by herself.

'So, any luck with the apartment hunting?' said Laura.

'Well,' said Bella, 'I got some good news today. I was waiting for you all to be here before I mentioned it.'

'You found somewhere?' said Sarah excitedly.

'I sure have,' Bella said smiling. 'It was so difficult to find an apartment with my budget. Rents have really increased. I thought I was going to have to move back with my parents for a few weeks.'

'So where's the apartment?' asked Kate.

'Willow Drive; it's just five minutes from here. We will be neighbours. I signed the lease today.'

'I know those apartments,' said Sarah. 'They are nice. My cousin lives there.'

'That's excellent news,' said Amy.

They all raised their glasses to Bella.

'So what is the apartment like?' asked Laura.

'It's a ground floor two-bed apartment. The furniture is a bit old but it is decorated nicely so it has a cheerful atmosphere,' said Bella. 'Anyone fancy shopping tomorrow? I need to get a few house essentials.'

'Sure,' said Kate, 'I'm free.'

'Sorry, Bella, the kids have matches tomorrow,' said Amy. 'That will be my day.'

'I would love to go, Bella, but Fiona's birthday party is on tomorrow,' said Sarah.

'I am in Dublin visiting the in-laws, so count me out too,' said Laura.

'Come on, girls. Let's get a photo of us all together in the apartment,' said Kate. 'Bella, you can have it in your apartment in case you are missing me.'

Bella was tidying up after the girls had left.

'I think the girls thought we had a falling out,' said Bella to Kate laughing.

'I know they were really questioning why you're moving out, weren't they?' said Kate. 'We should have made up a story.'

A week later, Bella was knee-deep in bin bags in her bedroom. She found bin bags the handiest to use when moving.

'How's the packing going?' asked Kate.

'I hate packing up,' said Bella. 'You wouldn't think you could fit so much into a little room.'

'I am going to be here all day,' said Bella. Before Kate entered the room, Bella had spent the last 30 minutes reminiscing. She would always do this when moving.

She'd start looking at photos and get totally distracted from the job at hand.

She had pulled out a photo of her siblings, Gavin and herself in Joan's house. They were all standing by Joan's Christmas tree. They all looked so happy. Joan used to say to them, 'Christmas is magical.' Joan loved encouraging them to get creative and had got them all to make decorations for her Christmas tree. Gavin had covered the tree with silver tinsel. They had such fun decorating and they all baked Christmas cookies together afterwards. Joan had taken them into town also that morning, and she had given them all some money to buy a Christmas present for each other. Bella laughed remembering the teddy bear Gavin had given her which was now safely stuffed into a black bag. She wondered if Joan and Martin's great nephew Gavin still had the red toy sports car she had given him.

So sweet, said Bella to herself. *I think he is the only guy to have given me a teddy. I never got one for Valentine's Day from any guy.*

Stop it, Bella, you are thinking negatively again, she reprimanded herself.

'Do you need a hand moving all your items this evening?' asked Kate.

'That would be brilliant as I definitely have a few carloads,' said Bella.

After a busy day of packing and moving, Bella and Kate were sitting in Bella's cosy apartment with a takeaway.

'I am going to miss you making me tea and watching all the rom-coms with you,' Bella said in a sad voice. 'You were the best housemate.'

She could feel herself starting to well up and quickly got up from the table to put the kettle on.

'I know, Bella,' said Kate assuring her, 'but you are not too far away, so I will call over plenty for tea and maybe some wine. It really is a warm and cosy apartment. You will settle in quickly once you get unpacked and make it your own.'

'Thanks, Kate, for helping me set up the TV. I would be lost without that.'

'Well, Bella, I have to go,' said Kate. 'I'll be up early tomorrow as Maia is moving in.'

'It worked out well with Maia moving in,' said Bella.

Maia was Kate's younger sister who had recently got a job in Galway. 'I know,' said Kate, 'it really did. The apartment is just too small to live in with a stranger.'

When Kate left, Bella started to unpack and make her bed. It was 3am before she got to bed. She really wanted to get her apartment in order before going to bed plus she needed to find her journal; this was a nightly ritual now. Bella slept peacefully as she was just so wrecked from the day.

Bella's phone woke her the next morning. Annie had texted to congratulate her on the new apartment. Bella had not seen Annie in a few weeks, but they would contact each other regularly by phone. Bella understood how busy she was now with the baby.

'Call in some evening,' Bella texted. 'I will give you the grand tour.'

'Will do,' said Annie, 'Take care, Hun.'

Bella got up and turned the radio on as the apartment felt quiet. She opened the food cupboard and took out some cereal. It was actually the cereal cupboard. Bella laughed to herself. She could now have an entire space dedicated to cereal—she wasn't limited to one cupboard for all her food. She could also keep her laundry basket in the spare room; it no longer had to be in her bedroom. She would be the only one messing the apartment now. She had finally said goodbye to the cleaning rotas.

Oh, the joys of having my own apartment, Bella thought.

Joan had always told Bella to look for the positives in every situation so she started to look at the positives of purchasing a house by herself. She made a list and it helped her to stay motivated and focused on her goal.

It will be easier and faster for the banks to approve my mortgage as they will only need to assess me. As I am single, I won't need to concern myself with my partner's credit history.

By purchasing a house on my own, I will experience more personal growth. I will become more self-aware and an expert in all matters, as I will need to find out how to do everything for myself.

I will be solely responsible for making all the decisions.

I will have more freedom over location and type of house I purchase. Also as I have only myself to please, I will not have to compromise like couples have to.

I know my own expectations, and I won't need to worry about my partner's expectations.

It is better to be living alone than with the wrong man.

The next week Bella rang her bank to see how much the bank would let her borrow for a mortgage on her salary. She then gathered all the documents she would need to provide to her bank—bank statements of current and personal savings accounts, payslips, and an income certificate. She then started the process of completing her mortgage application online.

Bella's friends and family were most supportive of her move, and she received many cards and gifts for her new apartment. Joan and Martin's wedding photo was now on her display cabinet in her sitting room along with other family photos and, of course, the photo of the girls from their pizza night.

Bella's mum had planned a few dinner parties in Bella's new apartment. Bella much preferred the drinks party as she was not the best cook and she rarely practised. She would never spend hours slaving over a hot stove as usually she was only making dinner for one. Bella loved having the second bedroom for any guests. It also came in handy for all her clothes and shoes. Bella had plenty of friends and family stay with her over the next few weeks, which helped her to settle in and feel comfortable in her apartment. Bella finally felt grown-up, living in her own place and being solely responsible for all the bills. To her surprise, she really loved living by herself. The Saturday morning lie ins were a blessing with no housemate to disturb her sleep. People would ask Bella if she got lonely living by herself.

'No,' she'd reply. 'You've got to try it. There can be a lot of positives to it, trust me.'

Joan used to say to Bella, 'You are stronger than you think.'

One crispy morning in early December when Bella came into the office, she found Emma busy typing away. 'You are early this morning,' Bella said.

Emma smiled, 'Yes, I have loads to do on my last day before my month off.'

'Oh, go on, rub it in,' said Bella. 'I need to get married. I would just love a month off work.'

Emma was wearing black skinny jeans and a tan knit jumper.

'Love the jeans; the walking has really paid off,' said Bella. 'You look so skinny; those green salads may have helped too.'

Emma looked down and said, 'Thanks, Bella, I bought the jeans at the weekend. I have lost a stone now.'

Bella raised her brows in admiration. 'That's fantastic,' she said. 'Well done. I just can't believe it is only one week to your wedding.'

Emma nodded eagerly. 'I am starting to get a bit nervous now. So are you bringing a plus-one then?'

'I am,' said Bella with a smirk.

When Emma looked excited, Bella raised her hands and said, 'Before you get too excited, it's not a man. Kate is going to come with me.'

'Oh, very good,' Emma replied.

Bella didn't want to go to Emma's wedding by herself. She just hated having to go to weddings without a plus-one. She asked Kate to go with her as she didn't know a lot of Emma's friends and she'd heard at the hen that most of them were in long-term relationships or married. Bella didn't want to have to walk into the church by herself.

She could hear Joan's words: 'Bella, embrace being single.'

But it was something she found hard to do especially when it involved weddings.

'Will there be any potentials there? Has Dave any single friends?' Bella asked tentatively.

'I have done the seating plan', Emma explained, 'and there is one singles table, so I will put you and Kate there.'

'No wonder I am single,' Bella exclaimed aloud. 'Just one singles table?'

'You and Kate will be fighting over the guys,' said Emma smiling. 'Any plans for the weekend, Bella?'

Bella nodded. 'I am going shopping for a dress for your wedding. Can you believe I still have not got anything?'

'That's not like you at all,' Emma said with surprise.

'I know!' Bella sighed. 'I am on this saving buzz for my house. I am so conscious of my spending now that I don't go into town much as there's just too much temptation. I'm also going to get a Christmas tree for the apartment.' Bella loved Christmas and decorating the tree. It was her favourite time of the year.

Bella's entries in her journal

Three things I am grateful for

Pizza with the girls

My apartment

Kate for being my plus-one.

Joan's wise words to me

Get creative.

Christmas is magical.

Always look for the positives in every situation.

You are stronger than you think.

Embrace your single life.

Someone I need to send love to

I am not annoyed with anyone currently!

Positive affirmation

I am so happy and grateful now that I am taking responsibility for my own happiness in life and I love my apartment. I accomplish with ease anything I set my mind to.

Small steps I have taken on my journey to purchasing a house

Advised Kate I am moving out of the apartment.

Found an apartment and signed the lease.

Moved into my apartment.

Found out how much the bank will allow me to borrow on my salary.

Gathered all the documents I will need to provide to the bank when applying for a mortgage—bank statements of current and personal savings accounts, payslips, and an income certificate.

Started my mortgage application online.

CHAPTER 7

A special ring

It was Saturday; Emma's big day had finally arrived. Bella spent the morning beautifying herself. She went all out. Hair, nails and make-up were all done professionally. Now she was putting on her new dress. Bella was really looking forward to wearing it. She felt more confident when she wore new clothes.

Bella had set up a monthly savings account with her bank. This meant when her savings were taken out of her salary, and when she had paid her rent and other bills, there was not much money left for her to spend on clothes. Her new dress for the wedding—a fitted royal blue midi dress—was a real treat for her. The colour really suited her tan. She paired it with gold high heel sandals and a gold clutch.

The doorbell rang, and it was Kate.

'Wow, I love your dress!' Bella exclaimed looking at Kate in wonder. Kate was wearing a lovely red cocktail dress.

'You look absolutely gorgeous, Bella,' said Kate in return. 'Your hair really suits you up. You look so elegant.'

Bella had got an up-style at the salon. 'I fancied a change,' she said.

Kate came close and said, 'Let's get a selfie of us.'

Bella always said Kate was snap happy. Bella rarely took a photo; she just loved living in the moment. Plus, she knew Kate would have the photos.

'I got you a bacon roll,' Kate told Bella. 'Let's eat before we head to the church.'

Bella smiled, 'That's great! It's like old times with the bacon rolls.'

They arrived to a packed church and quickly took their places.

'Looks like it's a big wedding,' Kate observed aloud.

Bella nodded, 'Yes, 200 guests.' She had a good look around and noticed that most of the guests were couples.

Suddenly people were turning around as the music started. Bella stood up turning her head and saw Emma walking slowly up the aisle. Emma looked absolutely stunning. She wore a floor length, off-the-shoulder, white chiffon gown. Bella thought the beaded sequins added a nice detail to the dress. She loved the flowing long veil. Emma was elegantly holding a posy bouquet of garden roses. She smiled at Bella as she passed by. Bella loved this part of the wedding where the bride would walk up the aisle to her Prince Charming.

When Dave placed the wedding ring on Emma's finger and Emma said, 'I do,' Bella could see that Emma was just glowing with happiness. Bella began to wonder if she ever would get a ring from her prince.

She started to smile to herself as she looked down to her middle finger. She remembered her 25th birthday. To celebrate, she had arranged to go for dinner with her family, and Joan and Martin. Joan presented a gift to her before the dinner. Bella carefully opened the red velvet ring box and could not believe what she was seeing. It was Joan's gold ring which had a green emerald in the centre and was surrounded by sparkling diamonds. This was the ring Bella had tried to persuade Joan to let her wear as a kid on several occasions when she was playing dress-up.

'Please, Joan, I won't lose it,' she'd plead. 'Joan, how come I can wear your scarfs and heels but you won't let me wear your ring?'

'Someday, Bella, I promise I will let you wear my ring,' explained Joan. 'Just not today. You will understand when you are older.'

Joan always wore the eye-catching ring. It had been her mother's. Joan said when she wore the ring she felt connected to her mother, whom she had lost to breast cancer when she was only 15 years old.

'I can't take this ring,' Bella said to Joan, vehemently shaking her head.

'You have no choice, Bella. I am giving it to you; it's your birthday gift,' Joan had said with a warm smile. 'I am getting old now and I am not sure how long I have left in this world, but I want you to have this ring.'

'Stop it, Joan. You are only 82.'

'It was such a special ring to me, Bella, as you know. It's fitting for you as you have the same birthday as my mother. I want to give it to you when I am alive.'

Bella's eyes started to well up. 'Thank you so much, Joan, I will truly treasure this ring. It's a special ring for me now too. Now, come on, Joan, let's go, or we will be late for our dinner,' Bella had said, changing the topic quickly.

Bella was so honoured to be wearing Joan's ring.

The church was beautifully decorated for the ceremony with fresh colourful flowers and candles. Emma had organised everything so well.

Kate and Bella helped themselves to the mulled wine and complimentary champagne when they arrived at the wedding reception, which was held in a beautiful castle. 'The grounds are magnificent,' said Bella as they sat comfortably looking out the castle window. 'It's such a posh wedding,'

'How did Emma meet Dave?' Kate asked inquisitively.

'They met on Tinder,' Bella explained. 'They were only dating for six months when he proposed.'

Kate nodded and said, 'I suppose at our age, we know the qualities we are looking for in a man and after six months we have a good idea if we want to spend the rest of our life with them.'

'Very true,' agreed Bella.

'You can see by the way Dave looks at Emma that he just adores her.'

'Emma deserved to meet someone like Dave as before meeting him she had been going out with Brian for ten years and he cheated on her. She had been heartbroken.'

'Really?' said Kate. 'That's awful.'

'Yes, and what's worse is it was with her friend too.'

'Terrible,' said Kate. 'Some friend.'

'Emma had a lot of dark days at work when that happened,' said Bella. 'She was just so miserable. Over time though she learned to live without Brian and to forgive him. When she let all her hurt go, Dave magically appeared in her life. Well, all that and by swiping right! Ah, it's such a nice love story.' Bella's eyes gleamed with excitement.

Kate nodded and then said, 'Let's get a photo by the Christmas tree.' They walked over to the large lush green Christmas tree in the foyer.

'What a fabulous tree,' said Bella. 'I love the sparkling lights and all the colourful glass baubles.' She sighed with happiness. 'I love Christmas weddings.'

A bell rang, indicating it was time to go into the dining room for dinner.

'I can't wait to see who is at our table,' said Kate excitedly.

They walked in and sat down on the last two free seats at the table. Two of Dave's work colleagues were sitting beside them. Bella smiled at Kate when she noticed how attractive they both were. 'Hi, girls!' said a dark-haired, well-dressed man. 'I'm Matthew. Nice to meet you.'

Wayne, a friendly guy, spoke next. 'Pleasure to meet you. I must say, ladies, you both look amazing,' as he looked them up and down.

Bella smiled; she was attracted to Wayne straightaway— she loved his rugged appearance and his confidence. The waitress came around and took their orders. Bella and Kate found it difficult to eat as the men were so entertaining. Matthew and Kate seemed to click instantly. Bella ended up waltzing with Wayne and he was the perfect dance partner. They all ended up in the residents' bar together, tipsy and digging into a plate of ham sandwiches.

Over the next few months, Bella went on several dates with Wayne.

It was a Friday night and Wayne had treated Bella to dinner at a Michelin-Star restaurant. The food was delicious and the conversation flowed, and Wayne seemed genuinely interested. Bella felt the night had gone well.

The following night Bella had decided to have a quiet Saturday night in. Kate had phoned her earlier that day to see if she could persuade her to go out. Bella had spent a lot of money over Christmas, and with her strict savings plan in place she couldn't afford to go out two nights in a row.

Bella called over to Kate's apartment on Sunday evening to ask how the Saturday night out had been. 'So, Kate, did I miss anything?'

'No, not really,' Kate said hesitatingly. 'I don't know if I should say this.' She paused. 'I saw Wayne out.'

'Oh really,' said Bella surprised. 'Wayne told me he was not going out as he had to be up early for work on Sunday morning.'

'He was sitting in O'Connor's Bar with a blonde woman and I saw him kiss her. He didn't see me, but I could see him clearly. I am sorry, Bella,' said Kate. There was silence in the sitting room.

Bella asked quietly, 'Are you sure it was Wayne?'

'Yes, it definitely was,' Kate said sadly.

Bella exploded, 'The rat! Why did he have to lie to me?'

Kate could see the hurt on Bella's face.

'I just don't understand why he would do that,' Bella said in a pained voice. 'I thought he liked me. I would never do that to any man.'

Bella would never dream of having a few men on the go at the same time. However, in today's world, it had become acceptable for men and women to be dating a few people at the same time. After a while they would eventually decide who they liked best but in the meantime they would keep all options open. Bella thought the dating scene had become so competitive.

She would never put herself through this mental confusion, as to her, there would probably be certain things she would like about each man, and trying to make a choice would fry her head.

Bella liked to treat people how she herself would like to be treated. If someone was dating her, she expected them only to be dating her, and if that was not the case, she would just move on. Bella just didn't follow the crowd when it came to dating.

Joan used to say, 'Bella, you are unique. Never compare yourself to others or feel you need to follow the crowd. Be yourself when it comes to romance and never be afraid of rejection.'

'Did you hear from Wayne today?' Kate asked tentatively.

Bella nodded seriously. 'Yes, he texted me earlier asking how I was. He asked if I wanted to go to the cinema tomorrow night.'

'Are you going to go or say anything to him, Bella?' Kate questioned.

'No, I will just leave it, but I won't be meeting up with him again,' Bella said firmly.

The girls chatted for hours and polished off two bottles of wine. Kate tried to convince Bella to sign up to Tinder.

Bella shook her head, 'I know Tinder is how people meet these days, but it's just not for me.'

'Go on, Bella, just sign up,' Kate cajoled her. 'I've signed up, and it's exciting. I have met two men for coffee so far. Matthew from the wedding is still texting me too, so I might meet him for a drink as well.'

'That is great,' said Bella. 'Matthew seems like a real genuine guy and he sure was crazy about you at the wedding.'

There was no persuading Bella to sign up to Tinder as she just couldn't get the idea of swiping and then chatting with complete strangers. It just was not her. Bella considered herself to be a very open person to those who knew her, but she needed to meet someone in person first and then connect with them before she would start texting them. Bella was not good at small chat over text.

Bella liked it when a man asked a woman out on a date. She could never imagine herself asking a man out for a date as other women did nowadays. Bella would just prefer to stay single than have to put so much effort into dating. She sometimes wondered if women had ruined it for themselves.

When Bella chatted with men, they would tell her, 'Sure, you can always ask me out, you know, if you are interested.'

She remembered back to one of her previous dates. Bella had been parched by the time she arrived at the bar to meet her date, because of all her rushing around so as not to be late. There was no sign of her date offering to buy her a drink, so she went to the bar herself after asking him if he'd like a drink. He had said he would just have a glass of water as he was driving.

The next bar they went into, he still had not offered to buy her a drink. She had gone to the bar again and got a lemonade for him. That was it for Bella. She could not listen to him talk after that as the only thing she could think was, *How mean is this man!* He then had assumed Bella was not interested, and he started offering to set her up on Tinder. Bella put it down to another dating disaster and moved on.

Bella thought Joan had chosen wisely with marrying someone younger than herself as Martin seemed to keep Joan looking and feeling young. It was also a help when Joan was getting older as Martin was still very active and fit.

She loved the story Joan used to tell her about when she first started dating Martin. Joan was not sure she liked Martin and she didn't know how she felt about the age gap between them—Martin was nine years younger. Joan was deliberately over two hours late on their second date. She finally arrived for the date, thinking Martin would have left. However, she saw a fair-haired, dapper man waiting patiently and looking like a lost puppy. His teeth were chattering, and he was blue with the cold. It had started to get dark. Martin's eyes lit up when he saw Joan walking toward him in a red and white floral dress. Martin did not get mad about the long wait and did not even question it. Instead he pulled out a bag of liquorice sweets, Joan's favourites. She knew then Martin was going to be a keeper. Martin had passed Joan's test. Joan used to say to Bella, 'If he is a keeper, you will know when you find him.'

Bella realised she was now prepared to sacrifice finding love and going out less so she could purchase her house.

Bella pretended to be okay in front of Kate, but she felt betrayed by Wayne. When she got home, she closed her apartment door and just cried. Bella felt unlovable. *Everything about love is just so difficult*, she thought. Bella cried so much that night, finally falling asleep holding her journal. When she woke up the next morning she saw her journal on the other side of the bed. The upset of the night before came rushing back.

She knew what Joan would say to her if she saw her this upset. *Bella dear, you are a leading lady. Do not waste your tears on a man that does not deserve you.*

Bella then decided to delete Wayne from her life. She forgave Wayne as she knew holding on to any anger toward Wayne would only end up hurting herself.

Bella shifted her focus off men and back to her plan of purchasing her house.

Bella's entries in her journal

Three things I am grateful for

Joan's ring

Christmas trees

Kate for telling me about Wayne

Joan's wise words to me

Bella, you are unique. Never compare yourself to other people or feel you need to follow the crowd.

Be yourself when it comes to romance; never be afraid of rejection.

Bella dear, you are a leading lady.

Do not waste your tears on a man that does not deserve you.

If he is a keeper you will know when you find him.

Someone I need to send love to

I send love to Wayne for betraying me.

Positive affirmation

I am so happy and grateful knowing that I am unique, strong and independent. I respect and love myself.

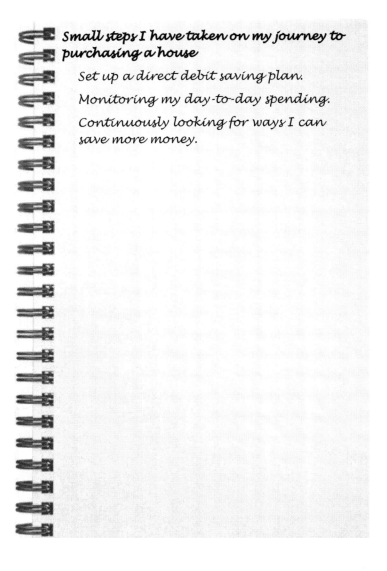

Small steps I have taken on my journey to purchasing a house

Set up a direct debit saving plan.

Monitoring my day-to-day spending.

Continuously looking for ways I can save more money.

CHAPTER 8

Perception and attitude

Bella arrived at work to see a big bouquet of flowers sitting on Emma's desk.

'Happy Valentine's Day,' said Emma, smiling.

Bella smiled back. 'Your roses are gorgeous. Dave is so sweet. Where is he taking you tonight?'

'We are just going for dinner, not sure where, yet. He is surprising me.

'I have some news,' Emma said mysteriously.

'News?' said Bella, getting excited.

Emma laughed, 'Yes! I'm expecting.'

Bella clasped her hands in delight, 'That's wonderful. I'm delighted for you.'

'Thanks, Bella,' Emma said with a smile.

Bella went on, 'I had my suspicions you might be, as some mornings you looked so sick.'

Emma nodded, 'I really was and so tired. I was dying to tell you, but I just wanted to have the scan first. Any plans yourself, Bella? Any dates?'

'No, not tonight,' Bella shook her head.

'Are you not hitting the town with Kate? Is there a singles night on somewhere?' Emma asked inquisitively.

Bella replied, 'Kate is actually going to one. She was trying to get me to go, but it isn't my scene, to be honest. I'm going to get a pizza for myself on the way home, along with a nice bottle of red wine. Then I'm going to watch a rom-com and dig into a box of chocolates that I bought for myself.'

Emma patted her shoulder. 'Sounds good.'

Bella was still implementing her strict savings plan. To save money she even started bringing in her own handmade soggy sandwiches to work. When Emma first saw her take her tuna sandwiches out of her lunchbox, she knew Bella meant business.

Bella was staying in most nights now, while her friends socialised. Whenever her friends would ask her to go on a sun holiday, a weekend away or to a concert, Bella would always have the same story: 'Sorry, Girls, but I'm saving for my house.' Sometimes Bella did question herself about whether this savings plan was causing her to miss out on life.

It was difficult for Bella to keep faith at times as part of her really did want to go out and have fun. Bella could still hear the negative voices in her head saying, *Bella, you will never be able to afford a house by yourself. Stop kidding yourself, it's impossible. It will take you years to save.*

Whenever Bella started to think negatively like this and got overwhelmed, she would say a positive affirmation to herself, which seemed to help change her thoughts. Bella also started to meditate every morning when she woke up. She found it difficult to concentrate, so she would just do it for ten minutes. After meditation Bella felt a lot calmer, and she got more clarity on her thoughts. This ritual also helped Bella to focus on the present. Living alone was also an excellent opportunity for Bella to learn about herself.

It was Sunday evening and Bella was just relaxing in her apartment when Elaine, her husband, Peter, and their kids, Chloe and Lisa, dropped in for a visit. Bella loved seeing her nieces. They always cheered her up.

'I have a present for you,' said Chloe handing Bella a shoebox. She had drawn a picture on the outside of it. Chloe was five years old and had always been very creative.

Bella smiled, 'I love the rainbow. It's so pretty.'

'That's you there,' Chloe said, pointing to a girl with long brown hair on the shoebox.

Bella's eyes widened with appreciation. 'Very good. I see we are at the park.'

Chloe nodded, 'Yes, and we are eating ice-creams.'

Lisa also pitched in. 'Look at the slide.'

'Wow, is that you coming down the slide, Lisa?' asked Bella.

'That's me,' said Lisa looking up at her. 'Open the box, Auntie Bella.'

Bella shook the box. 'What's in it?'

Chloe looked excited. 'You have to open it, Auntie Bella, and you will see.'

Bella slowly lifted the lid off and smiled when she saw a red heart. 'I love you, x x' was written on the heart. 'Oh that's just so pretty,' Bella exclaimed.

At that moment Bella understood how loved and blessed she really was. 'Thank you, Chloe and Lisa,' and she gave them both a gentle hug. 'This is the nicest present I ever got for Valentine's.'

'Auntie Bella has her happy face on,' said Lisa.

Peter and Elaine started to laugh at Lisa.

'She told me earlier I had my angry face on when I tripped over her doll,' said Peter.

'Now come over here, Chloe and Lisa,' said Bella.

The girls followed Bella over to a brown china bear sitting on the kitchen counter.

'I want to pick my treat from the bear myself,' said Lisa.

'You are so demanding,' teased Bella winking at her. 'And you are only three years old!'

Bella lifted the head of the bear and her nieces got excited seeing it was filled with sweets. 'Only one sweet for each hand. You know the rule,' said Bella.

The girls sat in the sitting room, eating their sweets and watching cartoons.

'Were you out last night?' Elaine asked before taking a sip of her coffee.

'No,' Bella said, shaking her head. 'You know I am saving.'

Peter was reading the paper but piped in, 'If I was single like you, Bella, and had no responsibilities, I would be out every night. Enjoy your freedom while you have it.'

Elaine gave Bella a look, and said, 'Wouldn't you rather go out instead? You may meet a man who has his own house and then you won't need to save for a house. It's going to be so difficult for you to purchase a house by yourself. Have you seen the house prices lately, the high interest rates, and the lack of supply in the market? Do you know when you get the house that it may not make you happy?'

Bella thought of Joan when she heard this as she would say, 'Being happy is a choice you make every day you wake up, and you need to make it a habit.'

Bella was getting plenty of advice on her life. Her friends were always saying, 'Bella, life is short, you should go out and have some fun for yourself.' All this advice just made Bella more determined than ever to follow her dream of owning her own house. She knew she was making the right decision for herself. She had been going out since she was 18 and she still hadn't met her prince.

Bella had lost faith in love saving her now. She kept thinking of Joan and how she would say when times get tough you need to keep the faith as there is always hope. Bella had a burning desire of owning her own home, and by now, she was emotionally attached to the idea. Being a Taurus, she was also very stubborn. As they say Taureans love their material goods!

Bella had started to watch any TV program to do with purchasing a house. She would sit in her apartment, visualise her dream house, and imagine what her life would look like. She would see herself living in her house, watching TV, sitting on her sofa in the sitting room, and even cooking in her kitchen. She would picture a wooden bench, colourful flowers and blossom trees in her garden. She would envision waking up in her house.

In the past, Joan was always trying to persuade Bella to try envisioning. She would say to Bella you need to visualise your dream. She believed in how powerful visualisation was, saying you could manifest anything in life you desired. Joan would always have a vision board in her bedroom, with her next goal on it. Bella never fully understood the visualisation process but she thought if she could see her house in her mind it might build her confidence and faith in achieving her goal. When she moved into her apartment, she decided to try Joan's vision board process for herself. She cut pictures from magazines of kitchens, gardens, and pretty much anything to do with a house. Instead of a board though Bella started to put the pictures on a full-length mirror that she had in her bedroom.

Bella registered with estate agents and started to view houses while she was renting so she could get an idea of house prices. She went online to apply for a mortgage in principle, so she could see the exact amount the bank would lend her—it was close to 200 thousand euros. Bella was open to living in the town or the country. She viewed houses in both locations. The only problem was there just were not many houses for Bella to consider in her price range. She could see the positives of living in town, as she was young and single. And, her commute would be shorter as work was located in town.

After numerous house viewings in town though, it soon became apparent that she was never going to be able to afford a house in town in her preferred locations. If she was to live in town, she would have to buy an apartment, not a house. Bella knew then that she was destined to live in the country.

As a child, Bella had grown up in the country, and she did enjoy country living as she loved the freedom. A house in the country would give her more space and her neighbours would not be too close to her. Bella did enjoy living in the apartment she was in, but she could only see herself living there temporarily. She could not envision herself growing old in an apartment. Bella did not like having no garden, as was the case with apartment living. There was no place to hang clothes out, and that really got to her.

Bella thought, at times, that she was turning into her mother. Her mum was obsessed with hanging clothes outside on the clothes line to dry. It was a sight to see her mother run if she had a full line of clothes out and it started to rain. It was like an axe murderer was after her. All anyone could hear was 'MY CLOTHES'. God forbid they would get wet!

Seven months later, in mid-September, Bella's phone beeped when she was at work. It was a text from Emma.

'Baby girl, Sophie. 8 pounds 2 ounces,' followed by a picture of a tiny baby wrapped up in a soft pink blanket. Bella smiled. She was delighted for Emma.

'She is so cute, Emma. Congrats to you both,' Bella texted back.

Bella thought what a lovely name Emma had chosen for her daughter. Bella's dad had said that he saw the name 'Bella' scraped into the steering wheel of a car, and that is how her parents picked her name. Her dad was obsessed with doing up old cars and anything to do with cars.

Ruth came toward Bella's desk.

'Good news,' Bella said happily. 'Emma just texted she had a baby girl.'

'That's wonderful,' Ruth said with a smile. 'Can you organise some flowers for her?'

Bella quickly got on her phone, and had a big bouquet of flowers and a pink teddy bear sent to Emma, Dave and Sophie.

Ruth and Bella had now developed a good working relationship. Bella had changed her attitude toward Ruth and started to focus on Ruth's positives. At first Bella was not impressed with Ruth's leadership skills, but then she began to understand Ruth's motives and the way she managed the team. Bella could see that when Ruth first arrived, the sales team were missing Nora; they were all guilty of comparing her to Nora.

Bella remembered back to the time of that rotten performance appraisal. She had been so upset. She could see the positives of the meeting now—she had been so dissatisfied that the situation had pushed her into taking action. When she was honest with herself, she realised it was true that she was not focused on her performance, and had not given her job the best effort she was capable of giving. Ruth had been right all along.

At the time, Bella had been lost in a world of her own, focussing on going out, drinking, and meeting her imaginary prince. It was only when she set her goal to purchase a house that she focused on her career, as she was dependent on receiving her annual performance bonus and getting a raise to afford investing in a house. She also wanted to have financial stability in the future. Bella had received her annual performance bonus at work every year since that appraisal. Bella was now excelling in her sales role, and Ruth advised her she should be aspiring to be sales manager.

Joan had always said she could see Bella one day in a leadership position. 'You should aspire to be a sales manager, Bella, as you do love to delegate tasks and you have the qualities—integrity, honesty, passion. But most of all you respect people.'

Bella had saved 500 euros a month. After two years of living in the apartment, she had now 12 thousand saved. Bella was proud of her savings, but realistically, she knew she would need another 20 thousand or more for a deposit as a lot of the houses were over 200 thousand. Bella was now 35 and getting closer to 40.

It was Saturday night, and Bella was having a quiet night in. She sat looking at her computer screen. She was reviewing her monthly budget again and checking to see if she had missed any areas where she could save more money. A thought came to her and she suddenly remembered Joan's words. 'Your parents are always there for you; don't be afraid to ask them for help.'

She then realised what she needed to do next: move back home to her parents' house in the country. It was just her parents and the terrier dog, Rex, at home. Moving home would enable Bella to save more money as she would not have to pay rent. It would also be a good opportunity for Bella to see how she liked commuting to the office every day. Her mother used to tell her how bad the traffic was, and it would take over an hour for her to get to work some days, even though their house was located only 30 minutes from town.

The next day it was raining heavily when Bella was driving out to her parents' for the Sunday roast. Today was the day she was going to ask her parents if she could move back home again. As she walked in the front door, she could smell roast chicken. Her mother, Veronica, was dishing out the dinner. She was a dark-haired, beautiful woman with a lean body. She had kind eyes and a caring nature.

'Just in time, Bella,' her mother said smiling as Bella came in. Her dad walked in and sat down at the kitchen table. He was a tall man with grey hair, an athletic build and he had always been very humble.

As they sat eating their dinner, Bella blurted out, 'So, I am thinking of moving back home.'

'What? Did I hear right?' her mum said, looking a bit shocked.

'Yes, I need to save more money,' Bella said hesitatingly.

Her father smiled at her and said he would love to have her home again. He saw this as an opportunity to help Bella out with getting a house. He was a generous man and would love to help Bella with her deposit, but he just didn't have the funds.

Bella never expected her parents to help her out with the deposit, as she knew they did not have much money. They had also put all their kids through college and any money they did have now would be needed for their own retirement. It used to annoy Bella though when people used to assume her parents would be able to help her out with a deposit.

Bella's parents were supportive of her decision, and her mum told her not to worry, they would not charge her any rent. The only question for Bella now was whether this would be good for her mental health. She wasn't sure how she felt about moving home again at 35, after living away for so long. She needed to change her perception and focus on the positives. Moving home was Bella's opportunity to save more money and it would move her closer to her dream of purchasing a house. With the right attitude, Bella could create her own success and change her life.

Bella's entries in her journal

Three things I am grateful for

Vision boards

My savings

My parents

Joan's wise words to me

Being happy is a choice you make every day you wake up, and you need to make it a habit.

Visualise your dream.

You should aspire to be a sales manager.

Keep the faith, as there is always hope.

Your parents are always there for you; don't be afraid to ask them for help.

Someone I need to send love to

I send love to Elaine for saying it is going to be so difficult for me to buy a house by myself.

Positive affirmation

I am so happy and grateful now that I have my house deposit. I feel calm and relaxed and I am fabulous.

Small steps I have taken on my journey to purchasing a house

Set a monthly budget and I am continuing to save.

Taking sandwiches to work instead of going to the cafeteria or eating out at lunchtime.

Limiting my spending by staying in and not going on weekends away or to concerts.

Visualising my dream home now that I have created a vision board.

Applied for a mortgage in principle to confirm how much the bank will be willing to lend me.

Researched locations to see where I would like to live.

Researched house prices.

Registered with estate agents.

Arranged house viewing appointments.

Saved 12,000 euros toward my house deposit.

Asked my parents if I could move back home. Thankfully for me, they said yes.

CHAPTER 9

Moving back to her parents' house

Bella knew it was going to be difficult to move back to her parents' house, as she would feel like a child again, living under their house rules. She started to wonder if she had made the right decision. Would her mental health survive this move?

'Is this the last of the bin bags?' her dad asked.

'Yes, thankfully,' Bella replied.

'I really don't know how you stuff all your clothes into bags,' Bella's mum said, looking annoyed.

Bella shrugged, 'It works for me.'

Bella had a lot more items now, as she had bought a lot of pieces of furniture for the apartment.

'Half of this will need to go up in the attic, until you purchase your own house,' said her mum. 'You just have too much for my house.'

Bella spent the day sorting out her old bedroom. It felt weird being home again, but Bella knew it would bring her closer to achieving her goal. The first few weeks went well for Bella, but the novelty soon wore off.

She missed the freedom of having her own apartment. Bella and her mum would argue regularly, mostly about the washing machine of all things. Bella would try to do all her washing on Saturdays when she was off work, but her mum was constantly washing, so the washing machine was never free.

And, since Bella liked to go places on the weekend and meet up with her friends, this meant Bella was under pressure to get her washing done on Saturday mornings, so she could hang her clothes out to dry. Drying clothes on a radiator was not an option in her parents' house as this was never done.

When Bella was a teenager she would often call over to Joan's house when she got annoyed with her mum. She started remembering Joan's words:

'Bella, stop saying your mum is grumpy. Sure, you have to do your house chores, it's all part of life. She is your mum, Bella, and one day she may not be here with you and then you will miss her so much, believe me. Be kind and grateful for your mum while you have her. There is no one that loves you more and she will do anything for you. Now go home and make it up with her. Here, take her this strawberry shortcake we made, as an apology, and that will get you in her good books again.'

Bella's dad was really easy-going and had such a gentle nature. It would take a lot to annoy him. The worst arguments Bella remembered having with her dad was when he was teaching her how to drive. Bella could not afford a driving instructor so she would persuade her dad to take her driving on the quiet country roads. Bella was a nervous driver and panicked if she saw a car coming behind her. She thought she would never learn at one stage and she started to convince herself she didn't need to drive.

I'll always live in the town, and there are buses, she told herself.

The only thing that stopped her from quitting was when she thought of Joan who had only learned to drive at the age of 60. Joan had regretted not learning how to drive when she was younger. When she did learn to drive she felt proud of herself for taking action and she would say to Bella, 'Don't die having regrets,' and would use the example of herself learning to drive.

As a kid, Bella had thought Joan was amazing, learning to drive when she was so old. Joan would remind her, 'You are never too old to learn a new skill.' Martin had bought Joan a red mini. Bella remembered Joan would often take her and her siblings out in the mini. Bella loved the little mini and the road trips. Joan's best friend Grace lived an hour away, and Bella and her siblings would often go in the mini with Joan to visit her.

Bella moved her TV into the spare sitting room, and she made the space her own. Her family used to refer to the room as 'Bella's little hideout'. She labelled it her 'positivity room' instead. She filled the room with everything that brought her joy and inner peace—from plants and photos to inspirational quotes. It was great for her to just have her own bit of space. She put up a few pictures and displayed some ornaments her friends had given her when she moved into her apartment.

She did not mind the daily commute to work while living in the country, and soon got used to it. Bella started to listen to motivational podcasts on her commute to work to help keep herself in a positive mindset.

One of the positives about living at home for Bella was that her mum always had her dinner ready when she arrived home from work. Bella was spoilt at home. Her dad would always ask her if she wanted a cuppa; she'd found someone again to make her tea. Unlike Bella, her mum loved to cook. Every Sunday was like Christmas Day in her mum's house. Her mum always had the roast dinner at 2pm without fail. It was not 2.05pm or 2.30pm; it was always 2pm sharp, and you had to be there for the 2pm serving.

Bella thought dinners tasted nicer when someone else cooked them. But that might have been due to her own cooking!

Over the next months, Bella stayed committed and disciplined to her savings plan. She went out a bit more on the weekends as she just needed the headspace, and she also wanted to give her parents a break. Their mental health was also being compromised with Bella back under their roof. They were used to it just being the two of them and Rex in the house.

Her parents were now back to wondering what time Bella would be strolling in when she was out with friends. Even though Bella was 36, her mum would still wake up as soon as she heard her come in the front door. Bella never remembered to take her heels off on entering. In the past Joan would say to her, 'You should wear slippers around the house.' She knew she had to invest in a pair now while living with her parents. She'd usually go straight into the kitchen and start devouring pizza or chips—any food she could find. One of the perks of living at home was that there was always plenty of food in the fridge.

The worst thing Bella found about living at home was the next day after a night out. That's when Bella really missed her apartment. She was no longer able to lounge around in her PJs all day long. Her mum never did that and had she seen Bella lounging around like that she would definitely have thought her daughter was depressed. Bella had to get up and be presentable for the Sunday roast. Her dad's running joke over the roast would be, 'You must not have drunk too much last night, Bella; you can still eat your dinner.'

If Bella was ever hung-over, the roast would be the last thing she felt like. In fact, she wouldn't feel like eating until the evening. Her mother would get annoyed when Bella would tell her she was not hungry for dinner and that she'd eat a chicken sandwich later. After a while though Bella noticed she did not drink as much while living with her parents. Her mindset was slowly changing. She also did not want to waste her money on alcohol or to suffer from hangovers. The funny thing was, Bella also noticed that the men she met out now were offering to buy her drinks ... just when she started setting limits for herself!

Most Saturdays, Bella would view houses, and her parents would go with her for support. As Bella's budget was limited, she would look at every type of house on the market, even houses that needed renovating. Her mum was horrified at some of the houses they viewed. Joan had always told Bella to be open to everything. Bella was taking on her advice during her house hunt and she would try and see the potential in every house she viewed. Bella had become obsessed with finding a house.

Sometimes it was challenging for Bella to take action on her goal. She used to get anxious about the small things in life, and would be fearful about taking action. This surprised people as she appeared to be so calm and confident, especially at her job. There were days when

Bella was feeling overwhelmed with the whole process of purchasing a house by herself. She was anxious about going to the bank alone to apply for a mortgage. She was afraid of all the questions the bank would ask her about her finances. She was afraid of rejection. She was also finding it difficult not to listen to all the negative media that was around about purchasing a house. The newspapers, current affair programs, and the news on TV were all reporting on the difficulties couples were facing getting on to the property ladder, communicating that it was taking couples years to save for a house deposit and house prices were increasing all the time. Listening to this, Bella thought she would be years living with her parents.

There was a lot to consider when applying for a mortgage, and to Bella, it was a huge financial commitment. Bella had so many questions: What type and term of a mortgage should she get? Which bank should she go with? What bank was offering the best interest rate?

With all this doubt and fear, Bella finally realised that the only way to overcome it and feel at ease was to get knowledgeable. She had to gain an understanding on all matters related to purchasing a house so she would feel confident taking action. Through her research, Bella soon realised that she could easily apply for her mortgage all online. She didn't even need to go into the bank or set up a meeting with anyone.

Bella spent hours researching. She decided to get an expert's opinion on applying for a mortgage and she arranged a meeting with a financial broker. The broker was just starting out in business and was offering free consultations. She also provided home insurance and offered other financial services, so it was also a chance for the broker to promote her services to Bella.

'Thanks for completing the questionnaire ahead of our meeting,' said the middle-aged woman, as she smiled at Bella. From the completed questionnaire, the broker was able to provide advice on the most suitable and competitive lenders available. She also provided information on life cover, income protection and home insurance.

Bella took out some papers from her bag and informed the broker why she had decided to go with this particular bank and the type and term of the mortgage she was considering. To her surprise, the broker agreed with her plan. Just getting that second opinion from an expert and having someone to talk it all over with reassured Bella. The broker was impressed with how much Bella had saved for her house. Bella felt confident and happy following her appointment. She was now trusting herself to make good decisions.

Through her research she learned that house prices had increased in the last two years. The Central Bank of Ireland had also introduced new rules for first-time buyers to further complicate things. Bella was now only permitted to borrow three and half times her salary. She would also have to have a deposit saved of 10 per cent of the purchase price of a house. By living with her parents, Bella could save one thousand euros a month and soon she had a total deposit of 32 thousand euros saved. She had reached her goal of saving a house deposit and was thrilled. Now that she had her house deposit, she went online and received her mortgage approval letter in principle from her bank. All she needed to do was find the house.

Birds were singing, and the sun was shining when Bella was viewing a lovely two-bedroom cottage on a hill, about ten miles from her parents' house. It was on the market for 175 thousand euros, putting it within Bella's budget. It needed some work, but she was willing to do some work on the house if required.

'It's just gorgeous,' Bella said to the estate agent.

She put in a bid of 180 thousand euros, but a few days later she was outbid by another couple.

Over the next few months Bella spent her Saturdays viewing more houses. She put offers on several houses but kept getting outbid.

Bella was getting desperate to find a home and she could feel the disappointment building up inside her. She chose to acknowledge her disappointment and to move on swiftly. She persisted with her search. She decided to focus her thoughts on what she had learned from each house viewing. She could see that each viewing was helping her to define what she was looking for in a house.

She remembered Joan would say to her you need to look for the good in everything that happens in life. Especially during challenging times and when there appears to be no hope. Joan would always say, 'Watch out for the rainbow. It will always appear.' Since then, whenever Bella sees a rainbow she smiles and it helps to remind her to look for the good and to have a grateful heart.

One evening, Bella announced that she was going out for a walk. 'Wait a minute,' her dad said, getting his coat. 'I will join you. It's a lovely evening.' Her dad had become her new walking buddy.

A few minutes into their walk Bella stopped at Joan and Martin's cottage. Bella thought the house was going down a bit now with no one living there. Ivy was starting to take over on the outside walls of the house. Bella remembered back to when she would go on walks with Joan as a little girl. Joan would hold her hand firmly and walk slowly so Bella's little legs could keep up. As the years passed, it used to make Bella feel sad watching Joan getting older. She could see her walk had begun to slow and she was losing her confidence when out walking. Bella used to call over to Joan and bring her out for a walk and this time she would be linking Joan's arm, helping her to walk. Joan used to say, 'A walk in nature does wonders for your mental health. Always try and go for a walk daily.'

'It's such a pity that they don't sell it,' Bella's dad said, looking at Bella. 'You could buy it then.'

'In his will, Martin had left the cottage to his nephew Sean in Canada. Yes, I wonder if Sean will ever sell the cottage,' said Bella.

'I don't think he knows what he will do with it,' said her dad. 'But Sean mentioned that his son Gavin is looking to visit Ireland again soon.'

Her dad started to look at the grass and said to Bella, 'I must cut the lawn tomorrow.'

'The roses are still in full bloom,' said her dad. And he picked a pink rose and handed it to Bella.

Bella's entries in her journal

Three things I am grateful for

My positivity room

Rainbows

Having saved my house deposit

Joan's wise words to me

Be kind and grateful for your mum while you have her.

Wear slippers.

Don't die having regrets. You are never too old to learn a new skill.

Watch out for the rainbow; it will always appear.

A walk in nature does wonders for your mental health.

Someone I need to send love to

I send love to my mum; my bin bags are handy for moving.

Positive affirmation

I am so happy and grateful now that I am waking up in my own house. I am passionate about my job and I am committed to my personal growth.

Small steps I have taken on my journey to purchasing a house

Moved back to my parents' house so I can live rent free.

Viewed various houses on the market.

Familiarised myself with the Central Bank's mortgage rules.

Applied for my mortgage online.

Had a meeting with a broker to get her financial advice.

Saved 32,000 euros, which is enough for a house deposit.

Organised my mortgage approval in principle from the bank now that I have my deposit

CHAPTER 10

Planning to build a house

Over the next few weeks, Bella plodded along in her struggle to find a home. She started to consider building her own house, an idea she thought over for a while before mentioning it to anyone. A lot of the houses in the country were massive mansions which were just too big for her and her budget. She thought the only solution now was to purchase a site and build a small house. She started to research the planning permission process online and made a few calls with her local planning authority to get more information.

One Sunday, as they were sitting down to the roast, her mum inquired how the house hunting was going.

'It's not,' Bella said looking disappointed and pouring gravy on her meat. 'There have not been any suitable houses on the market for ages. They are all out of my price range.'

Her mum nodded with a sympathetic look as she started to cut her crispy roast potatoes.

'Well anyhow, don't worry. I have a new plan,' Bella told them.

'Oh?' said her mum looking intrigued. 'What's this plan?'

'I know!' her dad said excitedly. 'You want to put a mobile cabin out into our garden.'

Bella laughed, 'No! That's maybe Plan C, though.'

Bella thought of Joan's words. 'Sometimes things in life don't work out as planned and we have no control over them. But remember: you always have options. You just need to persist and keep coming up with a new plan until you achieve your goal.

'Never quit on your dreams, Bella,' she would say. 'The universe will send you what you need; you just need to have unwavering faith to receive it.'

'Go on,' said her mum, shushing her dad. 'Stop interrupting her.'

'I am going to build a house,' Bella exclaimed happily.

Her dad raised his brows. 'Build? Where?'

'Well, that is the million dollar question,' said Bella. 'I don't know where or how, but it's my new plan.'

'I will keep an eye out and ask the farmers around if they will consider selling a site to you,' said her dad.

'That would be great. Thanks, Dad,'

A few months quickly passed by. Bella was continuing with her daily disciplines of saying her positive affirmations, meditating, walking, listening to motivational speakers, and writing in her journal at night. She was focused on living in the present moment and was trying to stop herself from worrying about the future. She was focusing on the joy in her current life and being grateful for what she had. In the past, Joan, seeing how anxious Bella got when she started to worry about her future, was always reminding Bella to live in the present.

It was Monday morning again. Bella felt good waking up now with a sense of purpose—it energised her. She was looking forward to the week ahead and continuing to take action on her goal of purchasing a house. She could see that her mindset had now changed. She was feeling proud of herself and could see the results of the action she had taken over the last few years. It had been worth it as having the money now for a deposit really comforted her. She felt like she was in a good place. Drinking less also helped Bella think more clearly, and she could see how her binge drinking in the past had affected her physical and mental health. Bella had learned also to love the daily traffic as it was a chance for her to listen to a motivational podcast or an audiobook.

Bella was sitting at her desk at work when Emma came in looking frazzled.

'I am late again,' she sighed, taking her coat off quickly and logging in. 'Sophie would not get dressed this morning, then she would not eat her breakfast. What a morning!'

'Relax, take a breath,' said Bella. 'I will go and get you a coffee.'

'You are the best,' Emma said gratefully.

Bella came back with the coffees and started to laugh. 'What's so funny?' Emma asked, confused.

'Your hair, there is something in it,' Bella said with another laugh.

Emma put her hand to her hair and felt something slimy. She looked at her hand and laughed. 'Blueberry yogurt!' She ran to the restroom to tidy herself up.

Secretly for just a moment, Bella was glad she had no kids. She didn't know how the working mums juggled it all.

At lunchtime, the girls headed out for a walk. It was the only opportunity Emma got in the day to fit in some exercise.

'Any luck with a site?' Emma asked.

'Well,' said Bella thoughtfully, 'I am viewing a site this evening after work. It's only ten minutes by car from my parents' house and it just went up for sale.'

'Fantastic,' Emma said with a smile.

That evening as Bella arrived at the site she could see the estate agent standing under a large apple tree. It was beautiful and it reminded Bella of Joan, who had taught Bella to look for the beauty in nature, and to appreciate the trees, the flowers and the birds. Joan loved growing her own fruit and vegetables in her garden. Joan would often bring Bella and her siblings on picnics in the fields near her house. She would pack a wicker picnic basket for them and fill it with sandwiches, fruit, cake and a flask of tea. They would all go on a nature walk together after the picnic. Every autumn they would pick the wild blackberries from the bramble bushes that were growing on the side of the narrow country roads. They would make delicious jam, and apple and blackberry crumble.

Bella could see herself building a house on this site and after walking around it for a few minutes she was ready to make an offer of 40 thousand euros on the site. 'The site is on the market for 45 thousand euros,' replied the estate agent, 'but I will advise the seller of your offer and get back to you in the next few days.'

The next day while Bella was at work the estate agent called to advise her that her offer had been accepted. 'Really?' Bella said excitedly.

The agent asserted and said, 'Can you organise the five thousand deposit, please, and drop it into the office? I will send you all the paper work.'

Bella, in a state of happiness, went to tell her friend, 'Good news, Emma! You will never guess it. My offer on the site has been accepted!'

'That's fantastic,' said Emma. 'It's time for a coffee break, we need to discuss this huge news.'

The next day, Bella dropped the deposit at the agent's office. 'Finally,' she thought. 'It's all working out now. I am supposed to build a house.' She felt so happy and relieved.

Bella was quick to share her good news with her friends and family, and they were all delighted for her. However, two months passed by quickly, and there was still no sign of the sale going through. She grew concerned as the estate agent still had her deposit and he was avoiding her calls. She could feel now that something was just not right with the site, and she was becoming impatient.

She called the estate agent again and he advised her that the seller was delaying the sale as it seems he now wanted this particular site for himself. While she was waiting for the sale to go through, Bella had spent her time consulting with architects on the cost of building a house. She learned building a house would be quite expensive. Bella planned to build a small two-bed cottage and the architect said if she wanted to proceed he could draw up the house plans for a fee of two thousand euros.

Bella's phone rang one cold day in October.

'Hi, Bella, I have some news on the site,' said the estate agent. 'The seller would like to sell you a different site. It's the site next to the one you have your deposit on.'

'I don't understand,' said Bella. 'He agreed to sell it to me.'

'He will sell you the other site at the same price,' the agent cajoled.

'Sorry,' Bella said. 'Why can't I have the site I have my deposit on? I love the apple tree on it. I don't understand.'

'Can you meet me this evening to look at the other site?' the estate agent said in a hurry. 'You should at least see it before you decide.'

'Okay, I will look at it,' said Bella, rather annoyed.

Bella met the estate agent. The meeting was brief as Bella only wanted the site she had her deposit on. There was no changing her mind. When the seller failed to persuade her to take the other site, he pulled out of the sale.

She felt like she had been kicked in the stomach. She felt angry with the world. The next day she called the estate agent's office to arrange to get her deposit back.

Bella was so disappointed, and she started to cry in her car, looking at the cheque she had just picked up. She was so sure it would work out this time. She hated having to tell her friends and family that this plan, too, had fallen apart. She felt like a failure. There were just so many obstacles in purchasing a house.

After four years of saving and with no house yet, Bella was ready to give up on her dream.

Staying positive was starting to get more difficult. This was the time she really needed to focus on her daily disciplines of saying positive affirmations and writing in her gratitude journal. The daily repetition of the affirmations helped her to move past the negative thoughts. She had also trained herself now to take six long deep breaths whenever she felt overwhelmed. The deep breathing helped to calm her mind, release her negative emotions, and stop her negative thoughts.

Bella went over the positives—*Thankfully, I did not proceed with drawing up the house plans or I would have lost two thousand euros. I am glad I won't be living next door to that farmer.*

Bella also learned to be kinder to herself when she experienced disappointment and to see every failure as a learning opportunity. She realised she needed to step back from it all and take a break. Joan used to say, 'It's okay to take a break and recharge,' when she saw her studying so hard before exams. Bella used to study in Joan's house as it was nice and quiet there.

Bella booked a weekend away to Lisbon with the girls to get over her disappointment and to recharge.

She felt energised again and ready to start the house hunt when she returned.

A few months later, Bella heard some news that was more hopeful. A local farmer was selling a site. Bella was interested in the site and she loved its location as it was close to a grocery store which she thought would be most convenient.

Bella viewed the site with her dad, and she put an offer on it. The offer was accepted, and Bella was over the moon again. Over the next few weeks her solicitor looked into the site and discovered a problem with the site boundaries. The solicitor advised her that she should not purchase the site. Her commitment to her goal was tested yet again. But this time, instead of becoming weighed down by the difficulties, Bella focused on the feelings of happiness she had when thinking of owning her own house one day.

Bella's entries in her journal

Three things I am grateful for

Positive affirmations

The roast

The weekend in Lisbon

Joan's wise words to me

Live in the present.

Look for the beauty in nature and appreciate the trees, flowers and birds.

It's okay to take a break and recharge.

Sometimes things in life don't work out as planned and we have no control over them. But remember: you always have options.

Never quit on your dreams. The universe will send you what you need, you just need to have unwavering faith to receive it.

Someone I need to send love to

I send love to the farmer for not selling me the site with the apple tree.

Positive affirmation

I am so happy and grateful now that I am creative. I am healthy and energetic and I am attracting good things into my life.

Small steps I have taken on my journey to purchasing a house

Viewed the site with the apple tree and put a deposit on it.

Looked at the cost of building a house.

Continuing with my daily disciplines of saying positive affirmations, meditating, walking, listening to motivational speakers and writing in my journal.

Taking the solicitor's advice and not purchasing the site close to the grocery store.

Took a break to get over my disappointment and to recharge.

CHAPTER 11

The Kennedy house

It was a sunny May day for Bella's 38ᵗʰ birthday. As she entered the kitchen, her parents started to sing 'Happy Birthday'. While blowing out the candles that adorned her chocolate cake, Bella wished to meet a man. For the last few years, she had been wishing to purchase a house. Bella was finding it difficult continuing to stay positive, and sometimes, she felt like she was never going to purchase a house by herself.

Bella started to question herself whether everyone's advice was right: find yourself a man first and then purchase a house together. This was going to be her new plan C.

Bella met her friends in town later that evening for birthday drinks to celebrate. She always believed in celebrating every birthday, and would take the day of her birthday off work to do something special. Earlier that day she had gone to a spa with her mum.

Joan had taught Bella to celebrate birthdays and be thankful for getting another year to celebrate. Bella was in a late bar with her friends, drinking a cocktail, and it was nearing the end of the night. A short bald guy walked up to Bella, and he started to chat her up. He made Bella laugh, and she realized how much she needed this. She was attracted to his bubbly personality and was enjoying his company so much she decided to wait a bit longer in the bar while her friends left for home.

'Happy Birthday, Bella,' Conor said and he leant in and gave her a birthday kiss. Bella was delighted. Things were looking up for her.

'I really enjoyed chatting. You were most entertaining and I loved hearing about all your travels,' said Bella.

'We definitely need to meet again,' said Conor. 'Can I have your number? I would really love to take you out for dinner for your birthday. How about tomorrow night?'

Bella hesitated for a minute, but then she could hear a voice saying, *Give him a chance.* Joan again! Bella decided it would be a good distraction from house hunting.

She smiled, looking into his eyes. 'Okay, but can we meet for a drink instead of dinner?'

Conor raised his eyebrows, 'Sure, we can do dinner another night.'

'Sorry, Conor, but I have to dash now as I don't want to be waiting too long for a taxi,' Bella said regretfully, putting on her coat.

'I will come with you and make sure you get a taxi,' Conor offered.

Bella had got very sensible now while living at home. She had to have her wits about her, since it was a 30-minute taxi drive to her parents' home alone.

The next day, she felt nervous as she was getting ready for her date. She was looking through her wardrobe and wondering what to wear. 'Oh, I will just go casual,' Bella thought to herself. She pulled out a pair of skinny black jeans and a red lace top.

Bella had advised her mum earlier that she was going on a date. It was easier to be honest, and she also needed a lift into town. Bella could never hide anything from her mum who picked up on secrets and knew when Bella was holding something back.

'You look nice,' her mum told her admiringly, as Bella entered the kitchen looking tall in her black stiletto heels that matched her clutch bag perfectly.

'Thanks,' Bella said with a smile. 'I recycled this outfit. I have not bought any new clothes in ages.'

'He has not seen that outfit before, Bella, so it's perfect!' her mum replied as she poured a gin for Bella. 'Drink this. It will help settle the nerves.'

Bella could see how excited her mum was that she was going on a date.

Bella had arranged to meet Conor in a bar in town. She had not been on a date in a long while. To her surprise, though, she found that when she met Conor, her nervousness completely disappeared, and she felt really relaxed, enjoying herself.

That night after the date, lying in bed, she thought, *All this personal growth and development is really paying off.* She could see the change in herself; she was much more confident now and relaxed too.

Her phone beeped.

'Hi, Bella, I really enjoyed meeting you for drinks and I am just checking to see that you got home safe. Night, night, chat tomorrow. Conor xx.'

'Hi, Conor. Yes, home okay. Thanks for the drinks; it was a lovely evening. Night, night.' Bella never used emojis.

Bella and Conor dated for two months. She really enjoyed their dates. Because Conor loved the outdoors too, they would go hiking, to the beach, and for long walks in the local parks. She loved having someone by her side to do all these things with her, and it did make them more enjoyable. He would often bring a little picnic for them. She saw how kind and sweet he could be. Once, he whisked her away for a romantic weekend in a castle.

He even met Bella's parents when he was dropping her home one evening after the cinema. When he said he would call in on her parents for tea, Bella thought he was joking, and said, 'Sure. Do, if you want to.' The next thing she knew, he was hopping out of the car. Bella's parents were a bit surprised when they came into the kitchen seeing Conor.

'Mum, Dad, this is Conor.'

'Nice to meet you,' her mum said with a smile. Her dad shook Conor's hand.

'Sit down there, Conor, and I will put the kettle on.' Bella's mum gave Conor the five-star treatment. The meeting went well.

'Your parents are lovely, so easy-going,' Conor told Bella. 'They seem like really genuine people.'

Bella laughed, 'Of course they are! That's where I get it from.'

The romance soon fizzled out. Conor got a new job, and he had to travel a lot for work. It became hard for him to find time to meet Bella, and he always had some excuse why he could not meet her. She just seemed to be an afterthought. She took it as a sign that he just did not care enough about her to make the effort and she decided to move on. Joan had always said to Bella that relationships are hard work but even harder when you are not right for each other. She knew the advice Joan would give her: 'Bella, listen to your intuition.' Bella ended the relationship as it was too much work trying to meet up with him.

She did miss Conor though and she was heartbroken again living at home, single and unable to find her dream home. Her parents were gutted too as they really liked Conor. They could see Bella changing her own house plans and marrying Conor, and then they would buy a house together. Well, in a fairy-tale ending they might, but not in reality. Bella looked to Joan's words to console her: 'Bella, remember you are never alone.'

With no romance to keep her busy, Bella became 110 per cent committed to purchasing a house again. It helped her to get over Conor.

Over the next few weeks, she set up another two house-viewing appointments with the estate agent but neither house was suitable as they both needed a lot of work. One house needed new windows and the other a new roof. She researched how much it would cost to renovate either house and realised she would not have the money for the renovations needed.

One day, Bella was sitting in the kitchen, reading, when her dad walked in.

He seemed very excited, 'You will never guess, Bella. The Kennedy house is up for sale.'

'Whose?' Bella asked, lifting her head up from her book.

'The one belonging to the Kennedys,' her dad replied. 'It's the bungalow close to the school.'

The house was just five minutes down the road by car from her parents' house. She used to pass this house every day as a kid going to school.

Bella always thought the house looked a bit out of place, as it did not face the road like all its neighbours. To her it had always looked like such a lonely house in a large green field. As it had always been a holiday home, there was seldom much sign of life around it. It was owned by a local, elderly couple who had moved from Ireland to Germany for work years ago. The Kennedys only visited Ireland twice a year. A neighbour used to maintain the house for the couple. The house was built on a one-acre site, so it did have a huge garden, but not much was ever done with the garden. No trees, shrubs, or flowers had been planted.

'It will be a great house for you, Bella,' her dad said with eagerness.

Bella shook her head, 'No, I don't like it.' She brushed it off without a second thought.

A week passed and her uncle John was home from the UK for a visit, staying at her parents' house. Bella's dad mentioned to him that the Kennedy house was up for sale. John was interested in buying a holiday home in Ireland himself, and the brothers hopped into the car and went to the house to have a sneaky peep in the windows.

'Yes, you're right, Michael. It is a beautiful cottage indeed,' John exclaimed. 'There is a nice big garage, and a massive garden. I could get a few sheep!' he laughed.

That afternoon John rang the estate agent.

'I am interested in viewing the Kennedy house by the school,' John told him.

'Okay,' said the estate agent. 'But, the earliest appointment I have is next Saturday.'

'Oh.' John was disappointed. 'That will not suit me, as I will be back in the UK. Hold on for a second. Michael, would you be able to view it for me please?'

'Certainly,' Michael responded cheerfully.

Bella's dad was really impressed at the viewing, and he came home, telling Bella all about it and urging her to come and see it with him. That evening, John decided to put an offer of 205 thousand euros on the cottage. His offer was accepted two days later. The Kennedys wanted a quick sale, and they were happy with the offer.

Bella's entries in her journal

Three things I am grateful for

Birthdays

Friends for always being there to help me celebrate

The romantic weekend I had in the castle

Joan's wise words to me

Celebrate birthdays and be thankful for getting another year to celebrate.

Give him a chance.

Relationships are hard work, but even harder when you are not right for each other.

Listen to your intuition.

Bella, remember: you are never alone.

Someone I need to send love to

I send love to Conor for not making the effort.

Positive affirmation

I am so happy and grateful now that I realise I am highly intuitive. I am worthy and deserving of love.

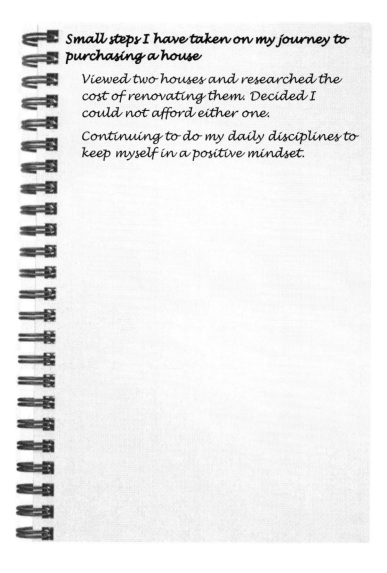

Small steps I have taken on my journey to purchasing a house

Viewed two houses and researched the cost of renovating them. Decided I could not afford either one.

Continuing to do my daily disciplines to keep myself in a positive mindset.

CHAPTER 12

Greenfield Cottage

One Saturday morning, in October, Bella was out for a walk when she heard something in the field. She looked over the stone wall. It was something black, curled up on the ground. Then she heard meowing and saw it was a little black kitten. She hopped over the stone wall and gently picked up the kitten.

'Oh, you poor thing,' said Bella. 'Come on, let's get you some food.' Once home, Bella brought the kitten into the kitchen and took some chicken out of the fridge. She put the chicken down on some newspaper, and the kitten ran over to it. He devoured it immediately.

'Poor kitten, you are starving,' said Bella. Just then, Bella's mum entered the kitchen and saw the kitten. She was surprised seeing an uninvited guest.

'Where did the kitten come from, Bella? He is not staying here.'

'I know,' said Bella. 'I just found him in the field. Someone must have dumped this beautiful kitten there. I had to bring him home; the poor thing wouldn't have survived.'

Bella took the kitten over by the fire to warm him up. Soon after the kitten was full of life. Bella tried to persuade her mum to keep the kitten, but she was not having any of it.

'Bella, it won't work out with Rex; he will kill him. Sorry, but the kitten can't stay here,' her mum said firmly.

That afternoon, Bella went knocking on the door of all her neighbours to see if anyone had lost a kitten. No one was looking for one or volunteering to keep him. If only Bella had her own house, she would have kept the kitten.

She was now tasked with finding a home for the kitten. Bella remembered the two cats Joan had. Their names were Sammy and Toby. Martin got them as kittens one Christmas for Joan. They were treated like royalty in Joan's house with their own special chairs and a cushion. Joan loved her cats, and when she passed away, Martin had told Bella that every night they would go up and snuggle on Joan's bed.

The cats were old when Joan passed away. A neighbour looked after the two cats after Martin passed away, but both cats had died soon after.

Bella pulled out her phone from her pocket and took a photo of the kitten. She texted the photo to all her friends. *This kitten is going to be so hard to resist,* Bella thought, looking at the cute photo.

Emma texted immediately. 'He is adorable. Where did you find him?' After a few texts back and forth, Bella was in her car driving to Emma's house with a little cardboard box sitting on the passenger seat. Bella knocked on the front door holding the fluffy kitten. She knew when Emma saw this vulnerable kitten, she would not be able to resist. The kitten was excited and he played around the kitchen. Sophie's eyes lit up; she just loved him.

Bella was right. Emma fell in love with the kitten, and decided to keep him as he would be an amazing pet for Sophie. Bella was delighted that she had found a welcoming home for the kitten so quickly. She was surprised with how easy it had all worked out. If only she could just do the same for herself.

The universe must have finally listened to Bella that night. It was Monday again and, soon after she arrived home from work, the phone rang. Bella's mum answered it. It was Uncle John. After a long conversation with him, her mum put the phone down.

'You won't believe it,' she said to Michael and Bella. 'John has just pulled out of buying the Kennedy house. He said the sale was taking too long.'

'But he only made the offer in August,' Bella observed.

'Did you not tell him the contracts can take quite a while to get signed in Ireland?' said her dad.

'I think he must have his eye on another property,' said her mum.

'It's an excellent opportunity now for you, Bella,' her dad said excitedly. 'You should buy it!'

Bella didn't say much about the house to her parents and went into her positivity room to read.

That night, after writing in her journal, Bella lay in bed, thinking about the house. *Should I at least view it?* She decided to see how she felt about it in the morning.

When she woke up, the Kennedy house was still on her mind. She decided just to go ahead and call the estate agent. She was off work on Friday and arranged with the estate agent to view the house. On Friday morning, while she was eating her porridge, her dad came into the kitchen whistling. 'Morning, dad.'

'What's the plan today, Bella, on your day off?'

'I am actually going to view a house.'

'Where?' said her dad, excitedly.

'Five minutes down the road. The Kennedy house.'

'Really? Are you really going to view it?' asked her dad surprised.

'Sure, why not? I may as well see what it's like for myself. There is no other house around to view anyway.'

'It's a fine house,' her dad said. 'I will come with you to view it.'

The Kennedy house was well-maintained. Bella could see this as soon as she walked in with the estate agent and her dad. Immediately she noticed the iron horseshoe hanging above the front door; she loved seeing this symbol of good luck. Bella was greeted by a warm and welcoming hallway. She loved the old timber chest of drawers and the plain arched mirror hanging above them.

'Great! It has a coat press too,' said Bella to her dad.

Her dad agreed and then pointed to the wooden floor. 'This will be easy to keep clean.'

'Yes, it's ideal,' said Bella.

The estate agent was quiet and told Bella to have a walk around the house herself.

She thought the three-bedroom cottage was most deceiving as it looked a lot smaller from the outside than it was inside. The cottage was a lot different from how she imagined it would be.

Bella walked into the kitchen. It was spacious, bright and airy and she loved the space as it had such a cosy feel about it. The wooden beams in the ceiling gave it character along with the wooden flooring. The kitchen was rustic with oak cabinets giving it a relaxed country feel. She loved the table with the wicker seating and the red and white floral cushions. She noticed the glass jug on the table holding a single white candle. She could picture the kitchen being the heart of the home as it just felt so warm and inviting to her. When she looked out the kitchen window she could see some beautiful hawthorn trees in the surrounding fields. She could picture the white flowers that would come alive on them in summer and the red berries in autumn and winter.

Bella smiled when she saw the bathroom. There was a green sink, green toilet and green bath.

It's just like Joan's bathroom. Real eighties style, she thought to herself. Green was Joan's favourite colour. She had a collection of green jumpers and cardigans; the colour really suited her complexion. Even Joan's bedroom was painted green. Joan used to say to Bella, 'When I am gone, and you see green, you will think of me.'

Bella started to laugh when she remembered the day she had got locked in Joan's bathroom. She was just six years old. Joan had to get Martin to break in the door. Bella was not scared though; she sat in the bath and waited as she knew Joan would rescue her. Joan had also promised Bella some chocolate cake when she got out if she just waited patiently.

Bella toured the rest of the house. The bedrooms were all tastefully decorated in neutral colours that made the rooms feel tranquil. It was a crisp morning, but the sun was out. The living room had two large windows, and Bella could feel the heat from the sun when she entered the room. Bella loved the stone fireplace and noticed a beautiful family picture above the fireplace on the mantlepiece.

The countryside views from the house were also breath-taking. Bella could see the rugged mountains in the distance. She finally understood why the house was built facing the way it was.

The cottage also had a detached double garage at the back. It was filled with peat that would be needed for the open fire in the sitting room. Bella was getting a good feeling, viewing the house. It was like it had welcomed her in and she was falling in love with this charming cottage. She had liked the other houses she had viewed over the years, but there just seemed to be something special about this cottage. She could not explain it.

Bella thought of the little black kitten and wondered if finding it had brought her luck. Had she now found her home just like she had for the kitten?

She walked around the house a few times while the agent sat comfortably on a rocking chair in the kitchen. She stepped out to the garden. As she was walking, she noticed a single white feather falling from the sky and landing on the grass in front of her. She smiled as she picked it up and held it in her hand for a few minutes before putting it in her pocket. Just as she did this, the estate agent came out.

'So, Bella, what do you think?'

'I love it,' said Bella, 'and I would like to make an offer on the house of 206 thousand euros.' Bella could see that the cottage would make a beautiful home for her.

'Excellent. I'll let the owner know immediately and get back to you,' said the estate agent.

Bella's dad was standing a bit behind her when the agent went back into the house to get his pen.

'Bella, should you not think about it over the weekend and get back to the agent on Monday?'

'No, Dad. I've made my decision,' said Bella. 'Besides, I need to act fast before someone else sees it on the market.'

Bella had not seen the potential of the house before she viewed it. But now she thought if families actually viewed the house, they would snap it up. Bella was already thinking about what she could do with the cottage if she owned it.

The weekend passed slowly, and Bella didn't hold out much hope of her offer being accepted. She was waiting again for another bidder to come in or for the seller to look for more money. She called the estate agent on Monday evening for an update and could barely believe it when the estate agent said he was just about to call her. He was now congratulating her, saying the Kennedys had accepted her offer.

'Really?' said Bella, excitedly. She did not fully believe what she had just heard. 'Thank you. I am so happy!'

Bella got off the phone and went into the living room to her parents. 'Good news,' she said smiling. 'They have accepted my offer.'

'Oh, Bella, I am delighted for you,' said her dad jumping up from his armchair and spilling his tea with the excitement. 'That cottage is perfect for you and I just know you will be so happy living there.'

'That's wonderful!' said her mum, smiling and giving her a big warm hug.

'Bella, you don't seem too excited,' said her dad.

'She is still in shock,' said her mum.

'I am excited, but I suppose until I have the keys in my hands, I don't want to get my hopes up. Remember, when I thought I had purchased the site?' reminded Bella.

'I have a good feeling about this cottage, Bella,' said her dad. 'It will work out this time.'

'Come on, Bella. Let's have a glass of wine to celebrate,' said her mum, holding up a bottle of white wine.

The next morning Bella contacted her bank to advise them that her offer had been accepted. She then contacted her solicitor. She arranged for a valuation to be carried out on the property. Things progressed quickly with the house as legally it was a very straightforward purchase. Bella got an engineer to do a report for her on the condition of the house, and she was grateful he found no issues with the structure. The interior and exterior were all in good condition. As Bella already had her mortgage in principle, there was no delay in receiving the mortgage funds from her bank. Her solicitor kept her well informed on how the sale was progressing and Bella was delighted when she signed the contract and was now the registered owner of the property. All in all, the whole transaction flowed smoothly; it was effortless.

The house sale went through in March, five months after Bella had made her offer on the house. She was thrilled one day when she passed by the cottage on her way to Elaine's house and saw the *Sale Agreed* sign on the lawn.

The day Bella picked up the keys to her house was such a surreal experience. She remembered Joan's words: 'You will see. It was worth the wait.'

She was the happiest she had been for years. She felt so proud of herself now that she had achieved her dream. She was also a little nervous as she had committed to paying a mortgage over a term of 25 years.

Every penny she had saved for her house over the years had been worth it. Every night out she missed and every sun holiday she chose not to take could not compare now to finally having her house. What a joyous feeling it gave her.

Bella cried on her way home, but this time they were tears of happiness and relief. Her determination and patience had paid off. She finally had the house she had visualised and dreamt about. She could hear Joan's voice: *You need to celebrate.*

She had just parked up at her cottage when her parents, Elaine and Peter, and their girls arrived to see her purchase. It was not long before her two nieces were running around the house like lunatics. They were so excited to be in Auntie Bella's new home. They had already picked out the bedroom they would sleep in for their planned sleepover.

'Where is the bear?' said Chloe, walking into the kitchen.

'He has not moved in yet,' said Bella, laughing. Bella then reached into her handbag and pulled out two lollipops for her nieces.

'Look, Auntie Bella, at the flowers,' said Lisa.

Bella walked over to the bouquet of flowers on the kitchen counter wondering where they had come from. She spotted a card attached. *Best of luck in your new home, Bella. Wishing you health and happiness. Love, the Kennedys.*

They are so kind, thought Bella. *What a lovely gesture.*

Just then the doorbell rang, and Una walked in.

'You'll have to start locking the door, Bella. Anyone could walk in,' said her younger sister with a grin.

'What a surprise, Una! I was not expecting you.'

'I had to come and see this place. It's a beautiful cottage. Congrats. You did well,' she said.

Bella's mother cracked opened the champagne that night, and the house was christened. Bella happily announced to her family that she was naming her house Greenfield Cottage.

The next morning at her parents' house, Bella woke up early and jumped out of bed. She was looking forward to cleaning her cottage.

Bella entered the kitchen. 'Wonderful, Mum, a fry; I thought I could smell it.' Bella's stomach rumbled as she caught sight of the eggs, bacon and sausages cooking in the pan.

After breakfast, they drove to Bella's house. Her mum and Una had offered to give her a hand with the cleaning. 'Okay, who is cleaning what space?' asked Bella, taking control of the cleaning tasks. Una was first to volunteer to clean the bathroom. Bella was delighted as she thought this would be the worst cleaning job.

'Your bathroom smells like Joan,' observed Una.

Bella laughed. 'It must be the lavender soap I put in it earlier.'

Bella's mother started to clean the kitchen. Bella started to wash the windows inside and outside.

From looking around all the rooms, Bella knew she would need to purchase some furnishings. She was grateful the Kennedys had left her the beds and the kitchen table and chairs. Even though the house was close to 40 years old it was in excellent condition. The kitchen was like new as it had barely been used.

It was a busy day of cleaning, and Bella even found jobs for her nieces to do when they visited. It became a real family effort. Una put on her playlist during the clean, filling the cottage with music. It reminded Bella of Joan's house.

The next day after cleaning her home, Bella and her mum went furniture shopping. After paying her house deposit, stamp duty, legal fees and insurance cover, Bella had a little bit of money left over for some furniture. Bella purchased a lovely rose pink velvet sofa and cream cushions for the sitting room. Elaine gave Bella an old, white, wooden coffee table, and a floor lamp to complete the room. Bella picked up two cheap bar stools for the kitchen in a local second-hand market and created her own little breakfast bar. In the past, Bella would visit the markets with Joan, for Joan used to love picking up furniture there. She used to say to Bella that old furniture had more character than new furniture. The best part about Bella's house was that it was close to her parents' house. It was comforting for Bella, knowing she would still be able to enjoy her mum's dinners.

Even though Bella had her own house now, she continued to live with her parents as she had to wait a few weeks for her new sofa to be delivered. Also since her house had not been lived in for a while, it was quite cold.

One evening, Bella's brother Alan called around to see her new house. 'Welcome to the mortgage club,' said Alan.

'I would prefer to have a mortgage than still be renting,' said Bella. 'You know, the cost of my mortgage repayments now are less than what I was paying for my two-bed apartment in town.'

'Yes, I would believe it well,' said Alan. 'Landlords keep putting up the rents. Anyhow, Bella, when are you moving in? You must have it so good at home now, you don't want to move out,' he teased.

'In two weeks,' said Bella.

She suddenly questioned herself: *Oh my God! Am I afraid to move out after three years of living with my parents?* Bella wondered whether she would be comfortable living by herself again as she was so used to having company once more. She heard Joan's words again: *Bella, remember you are never alone.*

Bella's entries in her journal

Three things I am grateful for

A home for myself and the kitten

Greenfield Cottage

Support from my family especially with the cleaning

Joan's wise words to me

You will see it was worth the wait.

An angel is near.

Visit the market.

You need to celebrate.

Bella, remember: you are never alone.

Someone I need to send love to

I send love to Mum for not letting me keep the kitten.

Positive affirmation

I am so happy and grateful for being alive, having loving relationships and being respected. I love making decisions and living in my house.

Small steps I have taken on my journey to purchasing a house

Viewed Greenfield Cottage and made an offer. When my offer was accepted, I advised my bank and solicitor.

Organised a valuation report.

Hired an engineer to complete an engineer's report on the condition of the house.

Arranged life cover and home insurance.

Signed the contracts.

Goal achieved. Finally, I have collected my house keys. Let the celebrations begin!.

Chapter 13

Life is short

B ella wanted to celebrate achieving her goal and her plan now was to throw herself a house-warming party. She invited her family and close friends to the party. She had not moved into her house yet as she was still waiting for her sofa. She thought the sitting room without a sofa would be just perfect for the party as it would allow plenty of space in the room for dancing. She would then put some wooden stools along the sides of the room for her guests to sit on.

Bella was also afraid if she didn't set a date for the party she would end up not organising one. She would probably keep putting the party off until she painted the rooms, got new carpet and found the right furnishings for her home. She was such a perfectionist!

She knew she had to keep things simple for the party as it was just herself entertaining her guests.

On the day of the party, the caterers arrived with the food. Bella had ordered curry, beef stroganoff, and lasagne.

'God, I really hope people turn up. I've got so much food!'

'Don't worry, Bella; it will all be eaten and if not you can freeze any leftovers,' said Una.

There were also two big bowls of mixed salad her mum had made. For dessert Una made a strawberry cheesecake and an apple pie. At about 3pm, the first guests started to arrive. Una who was an expert at making cocktails took responsibility for the makeshift bar Bella had set up in the sitting room. Alan was the designated DJ. Kate, Amy, Laura and Sarah all arrived together with their partners.

Kate had brought Matthew along to the party. They had been going out exclusively now for two years and Matthew had just moved into the apartment with Kate. Bella observed how happy they both were together when she saw them dancing in her sitting room.

Not long after, Emma and Dave arrived. Emma handed Bella a card and a large box, wrapped in gold paper and tied with a red ribbon.

'Thanks so much, Emma. There was really no need to get me a gift.'

'I am just so happy to be standing in your beautiful cottage,' said Emma smiling, 'You really deserve it, Bella.

There were times, over the last five years, I was beginning to wonder if you would ever find a house.'

'Thanks for all your support, Emma, while I was house hunting. It meant a lot to me. I am sure you were fed up looking at the pictures of my latest viewing,' Bella said, laughing.

'Not at all,' said Emma. 'I loved hearing about your house viewings.'

Bella opened the box and started to smile. In the box was a lovely landscape picture of a cottage surrounded by roses and blossom trees set in the picturesque countryside.

'I love it, Emma; how did you know?' Bella was overwhelmed.

'I used to see you look at it in the shop window every time we passed by on our walk. The day you took a photo of the picture with your phone I knew the picture must be special.'

'Yes. I put the photo on my vision board. I did manifest the cottage. All I need now is to manifest the roses and blossom trees.'

'You will, in time,' said Emma smiling.

Bella had a busy but enjoyable night. She had not realised how much work was involved in hosting a party. She was kept busy greeting her guests as they arrived, giving them all a tour of the cottage, and ensuring they all got something to eat and drink. As the party went on late into the night, Bella had to cook more food as the guests were getting hungry again. They were all laughing when Bella burnt the pizza and set off the fire alarm. Bella's family and friends were glad she had made the wise decision to get the caterers in.

'I was only testing to see if the fire alarm worked,' said Bella blushing. Joan used to always say this to Bella: 'Before you move into a house, I hope you test the fire alarm.'

It was two weeks now since Bella had purchased her house. She was enjoying the feeling of owning her own house and she now felt ready to move in. One Wednesday evening, after a busy day at work, Bella walked into her parents' sitting room, finding them both relaxing in their armchairs and watching TV.

'I am just going for a walk. You coming, Dad?'

'No, Love, I am going to give it a skip this evening. I am a bit tired.'

'Okay. Did you go down to see my house today?' asked Bella.

'Yes, I was down in the afternoon, and it was lovely and warm.'

'Good,' said Bella. 'I hope it won't be a cold house as you know how much I love the heat.'

'We do! We'll save a fortune on our heating bills when you move out,' said her mum, nodding with a smile.

'To be honest I was actually sweating down there today,' her dad said.

'Jeez! You must be sick if you were sweating in my house!'

She then announced that she would be moving out that Friday.

'Friday? What is the rush, Bella?' said her dad.

'Well, they say it's good luck to move into your new house on a Friday,' said Bella. 'And, I feel now is the right time for me. Are you not both sick of me after three years?'

'No, darling,' said her dad smiling. 'We loved having you home again.'

That night when Bella was in bed, she awoke suddenly to the sound of voices. It was still dark, and when she looked over at the clock, it was only 2am. She started to panic as she sensed something was wrong. She could hear her mum and dad talking low next door in their bedroom. Before she could understand anything, the house phone rang. Bella wondered who could be ringing so late, and she feared the worst. It took her back to the phone call she had received from Elaine advising her Joan had passed away. Bella got out of her bed quickly, and as she opened her bedroom door, she could see her dad lying on his bedroom floor, holding his chest.

Bella knew it was bad as her dad looked so pale and was clearly in unbearable pain. Bella had never seen her dad like this. He was always so strong, never ill and he never complained about his health. She could hear her mum on the phone to the after-hours emergency doctor.

Bella's dad had been up late, watching TV. He had felt unwell and had developed a pain in his chest and was in a cold sweat. As the pain got worse, he went into the bedroom to wake Bella's mum. He knew he needed an ambulance. Her mum had woken up from a deep sleep and thought, at first, it was probably just indigestion, and he was being a little dramatic. Her dad was insistent though, and when her mum got up from bed to call the doctor, she could see how sick her husband was. As there was a family history of heart disease on her dad's side, the emergency doctor had advised Bella's mum to call the ambulance immediately and not to take any chances.

Bella spoke to the ambulance operator, while her mum tried to keep her dad calm. The operator asked her a number of questions about her dad's condition.

Bella's dad was 63 years old. He was always fearful about getting a heart attack as his twin brother Liam had died that way at 50.

On hearing the ambulance, Bella's dad seemed to get energy from somewhere; he rose from the floor and started to walk outside to the ambulance. Bella's dad knew what was happening. The ambulance driver brought him back into the house swiftly.

'Michael, we just need to assess you first. Sit down there on the chair.'

Bella waited in the kitchen while they were assessing her dad and realised she had better get dressed. Ten minutes later, her dad walked out to the ambulance again, and this time they were taking him to the hospital, and the blue light was on. The ambulance driver spoke to Bella's mum before they left.

'Yes, it looks like a heart attack. We need to get Michael to the hospital urgently.'

That night Bella must have broken every speed limit behind the ambulance driving to the hospital. Bella's mum was glad she had not gone in the ambulance as the paramedics had to revive Michael on the way to the hospital. When Bella and her mum arrived at the hospital, a nurse took them both into the emergency room. Bella could see three doctors around her dad's bed.

Bella stood back so the doctors could assess him. Her legs were shaking. She had not been in a hospital since the evening she had said goodbye to Joan. She began to think of Joan. She could see her smiling face; it comforted her. Bella was trying her best not to look upset as she knew she needed to remain calm and strong for her parents. Her dad could not say much with the pain, but as he was lying there he started pointing his finger up to the ceiling, saying he was going up. At that moment, her mum replied with a firm 'no' and pointed her finger down to the ground.

For a brief second, Bella and her mum started to laugh and her dad even managed a smile. Bella got the feeling that everything would be okay and she started focusing on seeing her dad well. She imagined going for a walk with her dad, him making her a cup of tea, him at home watching TV in his armchair, and him visiting her in her new house.

Bella and her mum sat in the waiting room while her dad was getting three stents put in. Bella started to pray, and she knew her mum was doing the same.

They were both so relieved when the doctor finally appeared.

'We had to revive Michael again when we were putting in the stents, but he is okay, he made it.' Bella and her mum were so thankful to the doctors. Her dad had been moved to a ward. Bella was so relieved when she saw her dad a few hours later, sitting up and eating cornflakes.

Bella was tired now and decided to go back to her parents' house while the rest of her family visited with her dad. As she walked into her parents' house, a wave of relief swept over her—her dad was still alive! It all felt like a bad dream. When she had left the house the night before, she really didn't know if she was ever going to see her dad alive again.

The next morning, Bella and her mum got up early to go to the hospital. Her mum was busy on the drive in, answering her phone as word got around about Michael's heart attack.

People can just be so kind and caring, she thought. *It's nice to know people are thinking of him, saying prayers and lighting candles.*

Bella could see her dad was much better today.

She could now understand why she had not moved out straightaway after buying her house—it wasn't that she had to wait for the sofa to arrive, as she had told herself. It was the universe at work, ensuring she would be home that night for her parents. It was all meant to be. She was in shock for a few weeks after the ordeal, and it changed her. She was so grateful that her dad had survived. Her dad was the main man in her life, someone who was always there for her.

A week later, Bella's dad was released from the hospital. He looked gaunt as he had lost a lot of weight.

Her dad did not want to talk about his heart attack and relive the trauma, but he revealed to Bella that a few nights before he suffered his heart attack he dreamt of his twin brother Liam saving him. Bella's dad accepted what had happened to him and was now focused on his recovery. He was grateful to be alive and he was doing well in his cardiac rehab.

Bella and her siblings started to get concerned about their own heart health with heart disease in the family.

'So, Bella, are you going to get your heart checked out?' asked Alan one day.

She thought for a moment and then spoke up. 'If you get yours checked out first, then I will.'

Three weeks later, Alan phoned Bella advising her that he had seen a cardiologist and had some tests done. The cardiologist advised Alan that he was healthy, but he would need to lose some weight, drink less, and avoid stress where possible.

So, now it was Bella's turn. She always avoided doctors whenever possible. She filled the doctor in on her concerns about her heart. Her blood pressure was normal, and she was a healthy weight, so he was not too concerned. He just advised her to eat healthy and to maintain her weight. Joan was right; she would need to eat her greens. Bella became focused on her health. She was so glad she had taken up meditation as she always felt less stressed after practising it. Bella had to stay focused on maintaining a positive mindset and avoiding stress where possible. She knew how dangerous stress and worry would be with heart disease in the family. She also knew she had to celebrate her upcoming 40th birthday well.

Bella's entries in her journal

Three things I am grateful for

My house-warming party

The paramedics and doctors for saving dad's life

My dad

Joan's wise words to me

Keep things simple.

Be thankful for every day you get.

I will always be there for you, Bella.

Live in the present.

Before you move into a house I hope you test the fire alarm.

Someone I need to send love to

I send love to my dad for scaring me.

Positive affirmation

I am so happy and grateful for my life and I make a conscious decision to be happy. I feel loved.

CHAPTER 14

A gold locket

As Bella got out of her car at work, she saw Ruth coming toward her. Ruth stopped.

'Congrats, Bella, on your new house,' said Ruth.

'Thanks,' Bella smiled.

'You must be delighted. I hear you are moving in this Friday. You can have the day off, if you'd like.'

'Really?' said Bella joyfully. 'Thank you. I really appreciate it.'

'You deserve it as your results have been outstanding this year. You've put in a lot of extra hours this quarter and it's much appreciated. I know your appraisal is not for a few weeks, but you will be receiving a bonus,' said Ruth.

Bella's face expanded in a wide grin. 'Thank you, Ruth, that's excellent news!' It seemed the happier Bella got, the more successful she was in life.

Bella and Ruth's relationship had grown in the last few years. Sending love to Ruth had really helped. When Bella set her goal of purchasing a house, she also started to focus on taking responsibility for her own career development. She knew if she succeeded with purchasing a house, she would not want to be struggling with the mortgage repayments, so she started to look at how she could develop her career and earn more money.

She also realised that when she was going out less on the weekends, she was more productive at work. She had become more confident and her positive attitude seemed to have helped her to exceed her sales targets. Bella also set herself an action plan for work. Bella took on extra projects to build on her sales skills and to gain more experience. She wanted to demonstrate to Ruth how passionate she was about sales. She needed Ruth to see her strengths and see how committed she was now in developing her own sales career. She was aspiring to be a sales manager and she was open to receiving Ruth's constructive feedback.

Joan used to say, 'When you work hard you will always be rewarded. Just be patient; the rewards will come.'

Bella no longer saw Ruth as a stern, cold woman. She was now someone she admired for her courage, vulnerability, and resilience. Ruth was in fact Bella's mentor at work.

Bella's perception had changed toward Ruth one fateful evening when she was in the office working late. Bella passed by Ruth's office on her way to the photocopier when she suddenly stopped, having seen something strange. She could see Ruth's light was on and through the glass she could see Ruth in her chair, but she was sitting with her head down on her desk. Upon a closer look, Bella realised that Ruth was crying into her hands. She hated to see anyone so upset but wondered if she should intrude.

Would Ruth appreciate Bella seeing her this upset?

Bella went back to her desk but something told her to return to Ruth. She pulled out a packet of tissues from her desk drawer. In the past Joan would regularly tell Bella to keep some tissues handy and Joan at all times would carry a tissue up her sleeve. Bella knocked on Ruth's door. Ruth jumped up immediately, wiping her eyes. 'Sorry, Bella, I thought everyone had left. You are working late?' said Ruth.

Bella handed her a tissue, nodding her head in response to the question

'Thanks, Bella. I am sorry. You should not see me like this. It's most unprofessional,' Ruth said, not quite meeting her eyes.

'Are you okay?' said Bella. When Ruth nodded, she continued. 'We all get upset sometimes. You are only human.'

'I lost it,' said Ruth.

Bella looked puzzled. 'Sorry? What did you lose, Ruth?'

'My gold locket. I wear it every day.'

Bella knew the locket well as it had distracted her from crying herself in front of Ruth during her appraisal.

'It's not lost,' said Bella. 'You will find it. Think positively.'

Joan used to say, 'Never say you have lost anything or you will never find it. Just believe you will find it and you will.'

Bella began looking around Ruth's office. Soon she was crawling around the office floor but there was no sign of it.

'Okay,' said Bella. 'We need to retrace your steps. Where did you go in the office today?'

'Everywhere,' said Ruth, looking hopeless. 'I texted Linda to see if she or anyone else had seen it,' said Ruth. 'Linda said no one had handed it in to her at reception.'

'Come on, let's look around the office.'

They both searched the cafeteria, the toilets, the meeting rooms, the corridors but there was no sign of the locket. An hour later, Ruth said, 'It's gone.'

'Maybe Eileen found it,' said Bella suddenly remembering Eileen would have cleaned the office earlier.

'Thanks for your help, Bella. It's late. You should go home.'

'No worries,' said Bella. 'Don't give up yet, though. It might be in your car. And Eileen will be in tomorrow morning so I will ask her.'

'Thanks,' said Ruth. 'You must think it's a lot of fuss over a locket but it is very special to me. My daughter, Kim, passed away eight years ago and I keep a picture of her inside it. She bought the locket for me for my 50th birthday. She died a month later.'

Bella looked shocked and sympathised with Ruth.

'You remind me of her, you know.' said Ruth. 'She had those same chocolate brown eyes as yours. She was just 25 when she died.'

'I hope you don't mind me asking, Ruth, but how did she die?' said Bella.

'She had got a taxi home from the nightclub to her apartment and this man she was mad after had texted her, asking her to call over to his place. She got into her car to go to his house and on the way there she crashed and was killed instantly. Kim had been drinking and she never should have been driving. She was not in her right mind. One mistake and now she is dead,' said Ruth. 'I have lost my daughter.'

Bella was trying to hold in her tears. It was heartbreaking, listening to Ruth's story. It was just so tragic. Bella started thinking back to all her drunken nights out and the risks she had taken herself, thinking she was invincible.

'Do you remember that Christmas party, when I thought it was a good idea to invite partners? The truth is, I only wanted to invite partners as it was my first Christmas without Kim. I really wanted to go and celebrate Christmas with the team but I didn't know if I could. I needed Patrick's support. I remember you walking in that night to the restaurant and we were all seated for dinner. I thought you were just so confident walking in by yourself. I was admiring you as you just seemed so independent and happy.

'Kim was always chasing after some man,' said Ruth. 'She always had to be in a relationship. I think she was afraid to be alone. Her partner of two years Colin had ended it with her and Kim was just on a destructive path after that … drinking too much. I tried to talk some sense into her but she just wouldn't listen to me,' said Ruth.

'If I am honest,' Bella said. 'I was feeling so alone that night, walking into the party when I saw all the couples seated together. I guess I must be good at hiding it,' said Bella. She was also remembering the words Joan had told her on the night of her prom. 'Stop waiting for a man, Bella, or you will miss out on life.'

'Patrick was so nice that night, to me and the team. He made a real effort to speak with everyone. He is my rock,' said Ruth. 'We are married now for 30 years. Kim's two brothers also keep me going. I focus on my work and try and live in the present moment. I won't lie though, Bella. Some days are really tough.'

'I think you are unbelievably strong,' said Bella.

'I would appreciate, Bella, if you did not share this with the team. I don't hide Kim's death but sometimes it's just nice when people don't know as they can treat you differently.'

'Don't worry,' said Bella. 'I understand.'

It was after 9pm that night when Bella arrived at her parents' house. She felt drained and she went to bed as soon as she got home. She could not shake off her conversation with Ruth and she started to pray Ruth would find the locket.

Bella could see now how blessed she herself was. No one should have to lose a child. She also remembered Joan's words: 'Bella, never judge or be too hard on people. Everyone, is working through their own challenges in life and everyone has their own story.' Bella could understand and appreciate this now more than ever. She had no idea what Ruth had been feeling that night at the party. She was just so focused on herself.

The next morning, Bella went to work at seven to meet Eileen.

'No, I didn't find a locket,' said Eileen. 'However, I do recall now that you've mentioned it, when I was vacuuming Ruth's office, under her desk, I heard a jingling sound in the hoover.'

'A jingling?' said Bella.

'Yes, I just thought I had vacuumed up a paperclip. Come on,' said Eileen. 'Let's check the vacuum.' Bella and Eileen emptied it out and after a few seconds of sifting through the dust they found the gold locket.

'It's a miracle!' said Bella. 'Thank you so much, Eileen! Ruth is going to be so happy.'

After washing the dust off it carefully, Bella left the locket on Ruth's desk with a note explaining where they had found it. Ruth was so thankful to Bella and Eileen and left them each a box of chocolates and a thank you note. Bella was so happy to see Ruth wearing the locket again.

Bella's entries in her journal

Three things I am grateful for

My career in sales

My bonus

Finding Ruth's gold locket

Joan's wise words to me

When you work hard you will always be rewarded.

Never say you have lost anything or you will never find it. Believe you will find it and you will.

Keep the tissues handy.

Never judge people.

Stop waiting for a man, Bella, or you will miss out on life.

Someone I need to send love to

I send love to myself for judging Ruth.

Positive affirmation

I am so happy and grateful that I am a sales manager and I manage a wonderful team that produces excellent results.

CHAPTER 15

The big move

*B*ella woke up excited as today she would be starting a new chapter in her life. She spent the day moving all her items from her parents' house to her new home Greenfield Cottage. She loved having three bedrooms in her house—they allowed her plenty of space for all her clothes and shoes. Even though she had not bought shoes in a while, she still had so many pairs. Bella always loved shoe shopping ever since the day Joan had taken her to get a new pair of shoes for her first day at school. Joan's dad had owned a shoe shop in the UK. Joan used to work there; she loved working in the shoe shop as she was a real people's person and loved chatting with the customers and hearing their life stories.

Bella dreamt of turning one of the bedrooms into a dressing room, one day. The scary part was that even after giving away clothes that no longer suited her, she'd still managed to fill the wardrobes in all three rooms. Bella wondered how families had enough space.

Bella didn't sleep well the first few nights in her new house. She felt a bit unsettled in her new surroundings. She could not decide which bedroom she would have as her own room so she decided to sleep a night in each room.

One night while Bella was asleep, she dreamt of Joan. She saw Joan walking up to her front door and pressing the doorbell. Bella could see Joan so clearly, and she seemed so happy. At that moment, Bella felt so calm and relaxed. After that night, Bella just felt Joan's presence in the house, and she knew Joan was reminding her that she was never alone.

Bella picked the front bedroom for herself as it was the warmest room of the three. The morning sun poured into the room. When she looked out her bedroom window she had the most incredible view of green fields and wild flowers. She also loved looking out at the horses galloping around the fields beside her house and seeing the cows and sheep grazing.

A few months passed by quickly and Bella was feeling settled and happy in her surroundings. At last it was time for her trip to Dubai with the girls.

Since her flight was scheduled for the evening, she decided to go to work in the morning.

'Stop looking at the time,' said Emma, smiling over at Bella.

'I just can't wait to finish. I am so excited.'

'Are you all packed?' asked Emma.

'Yes,' said Bella. 'My suitcase is in the car as I am heading to the airport straight after work. I am collecting Kate, Amy, Sarah and Laura on the way.'

'Are the girls all turning 40 this year too?' said Emma.

'Yes, Kate is 40 next week. I am still only 39 until next year,' said Bella. 'We always said we would treat ourselves and go to Dubai for our 40th birthdays. We are staying in a five-star hotel; it's going to be so nice. I have not had a holiday like this in years,' said Bella.

'I am so jealous,' said Emma.

'I am a bit nervous about the flight though,' admitted Bella. 'I've never gone on a flight longer than three hours. I don't like flying for too long.'

'Ah, Bella, you will be fine,' comforted Emma. 'They have movies on the plane; you won't even feel the time passing.'

Emma was right. Bella did not feel the long flight pass with the two movies she watched. She didn't know why she had built up this fear in her head about long flights. Bella was glad the girls had convinced her to go to Dubai with them.

Though it was a short trip, every day was packed full of fun and joy. Bella was grateful to her family who had all chipped in to buy her plane ticket for her upcoming 40th birthday. She realised that being single was also a blessing as she had the freedom to live her life the way she wanted.

Bella and the girls loved Dubai especially the sun, the beaches, the boat trips, the shopping malls and the scrumptious food. Bella was so grateful that her friends were with her on this dream holiday. The girls could really notice a change in Bella. She just seemed content, and they put it down to her purchasing a house.

When Bella returned from Dubai, she decided to do some renovations to her cottage. She had some money now for renovations, following her bonus from work and her habit of saving. She sat down at her makeshift breakfast bar in the kitchen and made a list of the priorities. Her main objective was to make her home warmer and safer.

The first thing Bella did was put an insert in the open fireplace in the sitting room as all the heat was just going up the chimney. Bella also installed an electric shower as having to turn on the immersion for hot water was really putting up her electricity bill. To keep the intruders out and the heat in, she replaced the old front door with a new one that helped to conserve the heat in the house.

Bella committed herself to getting all the projects completed before her 40th birthday. As Joan used to say, 'Life begins at 40.' Bella had been saving for her house for most of her thirties, and her plan now was to enjoy her forties.

Bella's next challenge was how she was going to manage her large garden. Looking out the kitchen window, she could see how wild the grass had become. It was starting to stress her a bit as she had never cut grass or gardened before. To make matters worse, everyone kept asking her what she would do with such a large garden as it would be difficult to maintain.

Everyone was giving her advice: you should get a goat, you should fence off a section, grow wildflowers, have a vegetable plot. Bella just could not decide what she would do, but she thought it would be a good idea to live there for a while before she made any dramatic changes to the garden.

Everyone was impressed at how fast Bella was getting the renovations done, and in a few months, the cottage looked even more beautiful. Bella could not do a lot of the maintenance jobs herself, but she knew she could always get someone to do them for her. All she needed was enough money to pay them.

Bella had learned over the past few years to look at her problems and work on the ones she could fix. She had learned to stop thinking about things she could not control and to look to the universe for guidance. Joan had always told her worrying would never do her any good, and if she was to attract more good into her life, she needed to be in the right vibration to receive it. Bella loved doing up her cottage and seeing the results; she felt proud of her hard work. She now agreed with Joan when she used to say to her that an orderly house signifies an orderly mind.

Bella started researching ride-on lawnmowers as the grass was growing quickly and the lawn was now covered in yellow dandelions. She figured she could either be paying a gardener to cut her lawn or she needed to learn how to cut it herself. There were so many choices of mowers and they were quite expensive. Bella had no idea which mower would be the best for her to buy. Her dad did not have a ride-on mower himself so he could not advise her, but he said he would go to shops and look at mowers with her. The house hunting was finished, but Bella was still keeping her dad busy.

One evening, while researching ride-on lawnmowers on the internet, Bella saw a video with a young woman cutting her grass. *If she can cut her grass, I can cut my grass*, Bella thought to herself triumphantly. The next day Bella purchased the same lawnmower she had seen in the video. She was so excited when it was delivered. She never thought she would get so excited about a machine. Bella sat on her new mower, and she started to cut the grass. She thought it was one of the best inventions ever and made grass cutting so easy and, surprisingly, she really enjoyed the task.

It was so nice to be out in the fresh air, and the place looked so pretty when the grass was cut. Bella loved the smell of fresh-cut grass. She could see now why most men prefer to cut grass than do housework. Bella fell in love with mowing her lawn. It made the girls laugh listening to Bella go on about how wonderful her new mower was.

The summer flew by in no time. Bella began looking forward to spending her first Christmas in her house. She looked forward to decorating it. She went shopping with her nieces and bought some decorations.

She decided to get a real Christmas tree. For Bella, the start of Christmas was walking into a room and getting the smell of the Christmas tree. There was a Christmas tree farm about 20 minutes away from where she lived. The previous few years Bella had always joined her sister Elaine, Peter and her nieces when they were picking out their Christmas tree. This year, she would pick out her own. Her nieces were so excited about picking the tree. They tied a red ribbon on the tree they wanted and Bella did the same. The owners of the tree farm had a beautifully decorated log cabin where customers would pay for their trees. Lovely Christmas wreaths for the front door were also being sold and she helped herself to one. Inside the lit-up cabin Christmas songs were playing. There was mulled wine for the adults, and hot cocoa and sweets for the kids.

Elaine and their mum decided that they should all have Christmas dinner at Bella's house to mark her first

Christmas in her new home. Bella loved the idea at first, but then she started to panic: *Who would do the cooking?* It all worked out—her mum cooked the turkey, ham and stuffing in her own house and brought it down to Bella's. Una made cheesecake and trifle. Bella was able to handle cooking the vegetables and roasting the potatoes. It was a delicious Christmas dinner.

Bella remembered how shocked Emma had been at work when she asked Bella where she was going for Christmas dinner.

'I am hosting it at my house,' said Bella.

'Really? That's a lot of pressure on you—cooking for everyone.'

'I know,' said Bella laughing. 'So, I'm making the guests bring the food!'

On Christmas day, it was lovely having her nieces and nephews at her house, playing with all the toys they got from Santa. *Christmas is just so magical with kids*, Bella thought. Her brother Alan and his wife Sandra had called down in the evening with Bella's twin nephews Rory and Ethan who were nine and her niece Marissa who was four.

For Christmas, Alan had gifted her a silver clock and a picture frame that opened up like a book. Bella had placed the book on the mantelpiece above the fireplace. To the left side was the clock, and on the right side, Alan had put a beautiful photo of the kids and Auntie Bella visiting Santa.

Bella's entries in her journal

Three things I am grateful for

My ride-on lawnmower

The beautiful photo for my mantlepiece

My first Christmas in my new home

Joan's wise words to me

Life begins at 40.

Worrying will never do you any good.

Stop thinking about things you cannot control.

Look to the universe for guidance.

Christmas is magical.

Someone I need to send love to

I send love to everyone who gave me advice on how to manage my garden.

Positive affirmation

I am so happy and grateful now that I am surrounded by love, and I am attracting opportunities into my life. I love renovating my house and mowing the grass.

CHAPTER 16

A home

Bella had been living in her house for a year and a half when an idea popped into her head one morning. It's time to get a dog! At first, Bella thought it was a crazy idea—she lived alone, and a dog would be such a big commitment.

Bella tried to dismiss the idea for a few weeks, but this was her heart's new desire. Growing up, the O'Sullivans always had a dog. Bella started to look at the positives of having a dog. She knew she would be okay with the daily walks. She remembered Joan's words: 'Pets are really good for your mental health; they bring so much joy to your life.'

Bella's mum and sister called over to her house for coffee and cake one Saturday and Bella mentioned to them she was thinking of getting a dog. Their faces dropped.

'A dog? Really?' said her mum.

'You should volunteer in a dog shelter to see how you get on first,' Elaine suggested.

Bella could not see herself volunteering. She thought about it for another few weeks and then started to research the different dog breeds. She was interested in the dogs that didn't shed much, as having dog hair everywhere was not appealing to her. She loved the cockapoo. She thought they were like little teddy bears and they did not shed. Bella also wanted a dog that she could take walking with her in the evenings. Bella had always loved Labradors. *They always have a happy temperament*, she reasoned.

She couldn't get the idea of having a Labrador out of her head. So, finally, she decided she would just narrow her search down to Labradors, and she would just have to live with the dog hair. Bella bought two books on Labradors and researched the breed. It was now late November, and Bella decided the best time for her to get a pup would be Christmas when she would be off work for the Christmas break.

One Friday evening, Bella was up at her parents' house.

'How was work?' asked her mum.

'Grand,' said Bella. 'I was doing that first aid course most of the week.'

Ever since her dad had the heart attack, she had wanted to get trained in first aid. Bella had also persuaded Ruth to get a defibrillator installed in the office.

'Very good,' said her mum. 'I need to do one too.'

'Hopefully, I will never need to use my training,' said Bella, 'but it's good to have. The instructor was saying on the course that only one in ten people survive a heart attack.'

'Yes,' said her mum. 'Your dad was lucky he had it at night when we were both here and there was no traffic on the roads. That night the ambulance was here in eight minutes.'

'I know,' said Bella. 'What would we have done if it was any longer with no first aid training!'

Just then her mum's phone beeped. Her mum started to smile looking down at her phone. 'Bella, look it's a Labrador.'

'Who sent you that?' asked Bella looking lovingly at the photo of the golden Labrador puppy.

'Carmel at work,' replied her mum. 'Her dog Macy had pups and I was telling her today you might be interested in taking one.'

There and then, Bella picked up her phone and called Carmel.

'Yes, Bella, I am looking for good homes for five adorable puppies. I have just the one in mind for you—a golden pup you will love,' said Carmel.

Right away, she sent Bella a picture of a golden Labrador, followed by a video of herself playing with the pup. Bella was hooked; she had to get her now. Bella arranged to call at Carmel's house the next morning to look at the pups.

That evening when Bella went home and turned on the TV, she could not believe the film that was on. It was all about a Labrador. She saw this as a sign she had made the right decision. Her parents said they would come with her to see the pups.

The next morning, Bella's phone rang early.

'Are you still going to look at the pups today or have you changed your mind?' It was her mum.

Bella's parents did not fully believe that Bella would ever get a dog. They could not imagine her with a dog. Her dad was dying for her to get a dog though, once she suggested it, as he loved dogs. Rex was now 14 years old, and he was slowing down. Bella's dad was retired, and he said he would be happy to mind the dog while Bella was at work.

When they arrived at Carmel's house to see the pup, they saw Macy sitting on the driveway. As they walked up the drive, she came to meet them, wagging her tail. She was such a lovely gentle dog, and she gave Bella her paw.

Carmel came out of her house, waved her arm and said, 'Over here, guys. The pups are just in the shed.'

As they headed toward the little shed, five pups ran out to meet them. They were each wearing a different coloured collar. The pup Carmel had videoed with the pink collar was the first to come up to Bella. She was gorgeous and Bella started to play with her.

'They are all adorable, Carmel,' said Bella's mum as she knelt down to pet the excited pups.

'Do you want one too?' asked Carmel.

'No, we have enough with Rex,' said her mum.

'How old are the pups?' asked her dad.

'Just ten weeks old,' said Carmel.

Bella had a brief look at the other pups but she had fallen in love with the puppy with the pink collar who came running out to meet her.

'So, Bella, have you decided which pup you will take?' asked Carmel.

'Yes, it has to be the puppy with the pink collar.'

Bella arranged with Carmel that she would pick the puppy up on December 21st. She had chosen a name for her already—she was going to call her Angel as a tribute to her guardian angel Joan.

When Bella left Carmel's house, she went straight to the pet shop to purchase a dog bed and some toys for Angel. Three weeks soon passed, and it was time to pick up Angel. Bella's dad went with her. Bella felt terrible taking Angel away from her mum. On the way home Bella could see the puppy was nervous and she got a little car sick as it was her first road trip.

Bella found the first few nights tough as she could hear Angel whining for her mum. Bella started on the puppy's house training straightaway. She had a crate for Angel in the kitchen. She had also bought a kennel for her and installed a dog run outside, but she didn't have the heart to leave Angel outside in the kennel at night. Bella wanted to ensure Angel got used to going in the car so she took her to her parents' house every day for a visit.

Bella's friends all called over to see Angel, and they brought gifts for her. Her brother joked, 'It's like you have a baby and your friends are coming over with gifts.'

Angel was fun-loving and energetic and brought life to Bella's house. Bella found it tough leaving Angel when she had to go back to work after the Christmas break. Angel was in safe hands, though, during the day, with Bella's dad minding her.

Bella continued to train Angel herself. She remembered back to when she was a kid and watching Joan train up Riley, their brown and white beagle. She had gone with Joan and Martin to collect their beagle puppy. Joan was very disciplined in her training with Riley and she would reward his good behaviour with some dog treats. From all of Joan's training, Riley was a most obedient and gentle dog. Joan would say, 'Dog training is difficult, and you need to be consistent.'

As a youngster, Bella would get bored of the training and just want to play with the puppy.

Over the next few months and with a lot of effort and persistence from Bella, Angel was house trained and on command would sit and give her paw. She also learned the trick of opening doors. However, Bella did not teach her how to open doors; Angel learned this by herself. One Sunday when Bella was up at her parents' house, having the roast, Angel was outside in the garden; the puppy had a habit of jumping up, trying to get food off their dinner plates. Bella and her parents were just eating their dessert and looking out at Angel when the Lab stood up at the glass French doors on her two back legs, wagging her tail. She then pushed the door handle down with her mouth and used her paw to open the door.

Bella laughed. 'At least someone will open doors for me now.'

Bella had booked to go to Edinburgh for three nights with her family. They had planned more family events, being so grateful to still have their dad with them.

As Bella walked Angel into the kennel where she was to stay, all the other dogs there started barking. Angel was terrified and her legs were shaking. Bella started to feel bad for having to leave her at the kennel. Bella quickly said goodbye to Angel, and when she got home, the house felt so empty without her. Bella had to leave her at the kennel the night before as she had an early flight the next morning and they wanted to settle Angel in. Bella really missed Angel in the house that night as she had got so used to having her loyal companion there with her.

The O'Sullivans enjoyed Edinburgh thoroughly and Bella loved having all her family together. She was so grateful. Joan had always said to Bella, 'Remember, you are blessed to have your family.'

Once the holiday was over, Bella went to pick up Angel. The young Lab was delighted to see her again.

Angel jumped into the car straightaway, and she could not stop wagging her tail. Bella always used to be so depressed coming back from holidays, but it was different this time because she had missed Angel and was glad to be picking her up. The welcome she received from the puppy was really amazing. Bella felt loved.

It was a wet cold Saturday. As Bella sat down on the couch, she noticed Angel looking restless. Bella knew she had no choice. She would have to wrap up and take Angel out for a walk. Bella was grateful for the waterproof clothing she had recently invested in.

'Okay, come on, Angel. Let's go.'

Angel loved their daily walks and the whole neighbourhood had got to know Angel. Before Bella got Angel, she would meet neighbours and they would say hello as they passed by, but with Angel it was different. They could not resist a puppy and everyone stopped to chat to them. Even people Bella had thought to be a bit unfriendly previously seemed quite congenial now.

Angel was just so good for Bella socially. Neighbours were now arranging play dates for Angel with their dogs. Angel thrived on attention and she would run around after the other dogs, so excited and happy. Bella thought she may need to look at getting another dog someday as she knew Angel would love the company while Bella was at work.

Before Bella got Angel, she never fully understood how much a dog could change a person's life for the better. The welcome Angel gave Bella every time she came home was truly amazing. No human was ever that happy to see you. Angel also sensed when Bella had had a tough day at the office. She would come up and give Bella a face lick. Angel loved playing fetch and Bella was most grateful for her large garden.

The sun was shining on Joan's birthday. Bella drove to the graveyard. She laid four yellow roses on Joan's grave and sat down on the grass.

Joan, I feel like I need to introduce myself to you again as I feel I have changed so much. You were always my mentor and I know I learned from the best.

Somehow though, when you passed away, my soul got lost for a while without you. I became too focused on my current circumstances and feeling sad and sorry for myself. I was not seeing the good that was present in my life. It was like I had wiped from my mind all the guidance you had given me over the years.

Then I got to a point where I was so dissatisfied with my life I finally had my breakthrough moment. I realised I was responsible for my own life and I needed to take control.

Making myself accountable to you and remembering your wise words helped me to shift my mindset. I discovered

I was able to raise my happiness just by the simple practice of writing my gratitude in my journal. This daily habit changed my world and it helped me to connect with you again.

Joan, I miss you so much, you are unforgettable. You were a true friend to me and you have always been a light in my life, guiding me. I will always treasure the sweet memories of our time together. I still feel your presence with me every day and I feel joy when I remember your warm smile, your gentle soul and your infectious laugh.

My goal to purchase a house was challenging and I am so happy that I have finally found a place to call home. I have learned that there is so much love and support in this world and when you change your attitude and perception about your circumstances you do really open yourself up to receiving the good there is in this world.

Most people believe they would not be able to purchase a house by themselves or even be comfortable living by themselves. I have learned this is possible and being happy is every individual's choice. Everyone really does create their own happiness. Even if you are living alone, there are plenty of positives to your situation, and you just need to be aware of them.

You have taught me to have unwavering faith even in times of uncertainty, and I have learned to put my trust in the universe. I have built a loving relationship with myself and I have a grateful heart. I am no longer worried if I meet my Prince Charming. I am so blessed to be surrounded by family, friends, neighbours and, of course, Angel. I often think if I had kids of my own, I would have missed out on the beautiful relationships I have now with my nieces and nephews. I love being Auntie Bella. I am just waiting for Auntie's Day to be announced.

I do not know what the next chapter in my life will bring, but life excites me now. If someone had told me, as a little girl, that I would be living by myself at 40 with a dog, I would probably have started to cry. Today though I would not change anything in my life as I wouldn't be me any other way. I have developed a growth mindset on my journey to purchasing a house. I have learned if you are single and you don't have a partner or kids, you just need to get creative. Angel is filling this gap and my house feels like a home with her in it. I may find my soulmate out walking my dog yet, who knows, but for now, all I know is I need a house to live in and I am happy.

My life is not perfect, but presently it's fabulous, and I will continue to think happy thoughts, no matter what my circumstances are. I have found the happiness within me.

By the way, I picked these roses from your garden when I called over to visit Gavin. The IT company he works for is setting up an office in Ireland, and he is going to be based here for a year. Mum has had him over already for the roast. She feels sorry for him going through the divorce. It does sound messy, but at least there are no kids involved. He is still as sweet as ever, a real charmer.

Bella's entries in her journal

Three things I am grateful for

> Carmel
>
> Angel
>
> My home

Joan's wise words to me

> Listen to your intuition.
>
> Pets are really good for your mental health. They bring so much joy to your life.
>
> Dog training is difficult and you need to be consistent.
>
> Remember, you are blessed to have your family.
>
> You are responsible for all your thoughts.

Someone I need to send love to

> I send love to Angel for making me go for a walk when the weather is so bad.

Positive affirmation

> I am so happy and grateful for how easy it was to train Angel. I love my home and my life is fabulous with Angel.

CHAPTER 17

Open the door

*A*ngel started to bark, and ran out to the hallway and stood beside the front door. Ten seconds later, the doorbell rang.

'It's okay. It's just the door. Relax,' said Bella. Angel was an excellent guard dog, always alerting Bella to any visitors.

Funny, I'm not expecting anyone, Bella thought and she looked into the peephole. A tall dark handsome man was standing patiently.

Gavin! Of course, it's him. He would have to show up on the evening I throw on my PJs after work! No makeup either, Bella muttered under her breath. She could hear Joan's words: 'Open the door, Bella. Don't leave a handsome guy waiting too long.'

She opened the door quickly, and smiled at Gavin. Angel jumped on Gavin immediately and then started to sniff him. Bella could smell his lovely aftershave from where she was standing.

'Down, Angel,' commanded Bella.

'Sorry, Gavin. I think she likes you.'

'She is okay, Bella. I love dogs. She is beautiful and so friendly,' he said as he patted her head.

'I am sorry to disturb you,' Gavin went on to say, looking down at her polka dot PJs and fluffy pink slippers. 'Were you in bed?'

'No', said Bella embarrassed. 'It's only … I am just out of the shower. Come in, Gavin.'

'I won't stay; I just didn't have your phone number. You are a hard woman to contact. I couldn't find you on any social media.'

'Yes, sorry, I am not into that,' said Bella. 'Here, I will give you my number.'

Gavin added Bella to his contacts.

'I was just on the phone with Dad this evening about renovating Joan's cottage. My company has offered me a permanent job now in Ireland, and I have decided I need a fresh start.'

'Ireland will be a big change from Canada,' said Bella, 'but you will love it. You already know that though, from all the summers you spent in Joan and Martin's house.'

'True. I have always loved Ireland,' said Gavin.

'The reason I'm coming by is I need to give you something. Dad completely forgot. Joan told him she had left a box up in their attic for you and to make sure you got it when you turned 40.'

'Really?' said Bella. 'What's in it? Joan never mentioned anything about a box!'

'I am not sure,' said Gavin. 'It's sealed up with a note on the outside that says, "My special friend, Bella." I didn't like to open it. I was going to bring the box over, but I wanted to ask for your help first. Would you mind helping me to clear out their house? It's still full of their belongings.'

'Is it?' said Bella. 'It's been a few years now since I've been inside.'

'Yes, a big clear-out is needed,' said Gavin.

'I can imagine—none of you have been over from Canada in ages,' said Bella. 'You must be getting sick of looking at the communion and graduation photos of the O'Sullivans hanging on the sitting room walls,' continued Bella laughing.

'Well, no, but I did remove my own photos,' said Gavin. 'They were horrendous! What were my parents thinking with those clothes and that haircut?'

Bella remembered she used to say the same thing to Joan about her photos and Joan would say, 'Bella, you are too critical of yourself. You must learn to love yourself.'

The two chatted comfortably for a while and then made plans for Bella to go over and help with the clearing the following day.

'Wonderful,' said Gavin. 'I will cook us dinner.'

'There is no need, Gavin, to go to that bother.'

'I want to. It will be nice to have a dinner guest, and we can catch up,' Gavin insisted.

'Okay, thanks. How does 5pm sound?'

'Super. Come hungry. I will have plenty of greens for you,' said Gavin smiling. 'I remember cabbage is your favourite.'

'Very funny, Gavin. I do actually eat it now, you know. I love it. I have changed,' Bella said laughing.

'Okay, it's a date. See you tomorrow,' said Gavin.

A date? Bella thought, closing the door. This was a strange word to hear; she couldn't remember the last time she'd had a date. Joan was forever trying to persuade Bella to go on more dates. With focusing on purchasing her house and living with Angel, she hadn't thought much about dating. Bella had accepted she would be single and was happy with it just being herself and Angel. She was no longer looking for a man to make her happy as she was already happy.

Bella picked up her phone.

'Hi, Mum. Gavin just called over.'

'Oh,' said her mum. 'Why?'

'Do you remember Joan saying she had a box for me?'

'No. Did she?'

Bella filled her mum in.

'He invited you over for dinner,' said her mum. 'Can he cook?'

'I don't know,' said Bella. 'Hopefully, he can. I don't fancy food poisoning.'

'Ah,' said her mum. 'I always liked Gavin. He is such a gentleman. That was a lovely bottle of wine he brought over for the roast. And he brought flowers. He is so thoughtful.'

'Yes, he is,' said Bella.

'I remember the two of you used to pretend you were married when playing house as kids. Joan and I thought it was so cute.'

'We did not,' said Bella blushing. 'I don't recall that.'

'I swear you did,' said her mum laughing. 'I was devastated when Joan told me he had married a Canadian woman. So young too; he was only 23.'

'You will have to make dessert, Bella.'

'You mean *buy* dessert,' said Bella. 'He will be comparing my baking to Joan's. Okay, I'd best go. Angel is jumping on me—she wants to go outside.'

Early next morning Bella woke up to hear the birds chirping outside her bedroom window. Saturday morning lie ins were a thing of the past now that she had Angel. It was like having a child. She could hear Angel moving around the kitchen, pawing at the door looking for her food.

When Bella first moved into her house, everyone said she should paint all the pine doors white. Just as well she hadn't—the pine hid the dirty paw marks. Bella couldn't imagine having white doors while living with a Labrador. Bella had been tempted to let Angel sleep in her bedroom but then thought it would not be fair on the Lab if she was away for a night; Angel would miss her so much.

As soon as Bella unlocked the kitchen door, Angel was jumping up and licking her face, so delighted to see her. Angel was never grumpy in the morning. She was a perfect housemate that way. Now, if she could only make Bella a cuppa!

'I don't believe it,' said Bella again. Angel had made a burst for the laundry basket in the spare room and now had Bella's dirty sock in her mouth. It was a game now to her. It was Bella's running socks that always tasted so good to Angel. Bella knew what Joan would say: 'You need to get her some chew toys.'

The day flew by, and Bella was getting ready for dinner.

Oh, what to wear? she thought, looking in her wardrobe. *I would love to wear my track pants as we will be sorting out the house, but I suppose I'd better make a bit of an effort.* She took down a black pair of leggings from the clothes hanger and paired them with a long red blouse and black belt. *Now all I need is my black ankle boots and I am ready.*

Gavin was busy in the kitchen when Bella arrived.

'Something smells good,' said Bella.

'Oh, it's just lasagne. I made it earlier and some lovely green salad for you.'

Bella sighed to herself, 'My favourite dinner: lasagne!'

'Sit down there, by the fire, and warm yourself up,' said Gavin.

'It's quite frosty out today,' said Bella. 'I love your log fire; it is so cosy.'

Joan used to sit by this fireplace for hours in the evenings, knitting. Joan had knitted so many hats and scarves for the O'Sullivans over the years. There was a lovely picture of Joan and Martin still sitting on the mantlepiece above the fireplace. They were standing with their arms wrapped around each other at the beach. They looked so content.

'So, a glass of wine, Bella?'

'Oh, just tea for me,' said Bella, 'I'm driving.'

'Go on. Have a glass; I can drop you home. It's only down the road.'

Bella paused. 'Do you not want a drink yourself?'

'No, I don't mind, Bella. I don't really drink too much.' Gavin placed a large glass of white wine in front of her. She could not remember the last time she'd had a drink as she had not been out in ages. She didn't like drinking alone in her house.

'Cheesecake,' said Bella. 'I forgot I left it in the car.'

Bella came back in with the strawberry cheesecake.

'It looks delicious!' said Gavin with appreciation.

Bella could see Gavin had gone to a lot of effort for her. He even had pulled out Joan's best white lace tablecloth for the occasion.

'Take a seat there, Bella,' said Gavin as he placed the mouth-watering lasagne on the table. Gavin had a way of making Bella feel so comfortable and she could relax and be herself around him.

'How do you like living at Greenfield Cottage?' asked Gavin. On his last visit, he had noticed the wooden house sign hanging by Bella's front door.

'I just love it! I am the happiest I have ever been, living there. It's just perfect for me.'

'It really does look amazing,' said Gavin. 'You should be very proud.'

'Thanks, you are so sweet,' said Bella blushing.

'I love your big green garden too,' said Gavin. 'It's so nice to have a bit of space.'

'I do need to plant some trees for a bit of shelter as it can feel very open on a windy day,' remarked Bella. 'Some roses might be nice too.'

'I can plant some for you, Bella. What are you thinking of planting?'

'I would love some cherry blossom trees and an apple tree,' she replied.

'Let me know when you want to plant them,' said Gavin.

'Brilliant! I thought I would have to get a gardener,' said Bella with appreciation.

Bella filled Gavin in on the challenges she'd had purchasing a house.

'I really admire you,' said Gavin. 'You are one determined and resilient woman. I always knew that about you since the night we all went camping out in Joan's back garden. I remember Alan, Elaine, Una, and I had all come back into the house as we were freezing and it started to get so windy outside. Joan was trying to persuade you to come inside with the rest of us but you wouldn't. We could not believe you spent the night out there by yourself!'

'And, I couldn't believe you all went inside!' said Bella laughing. 'We were meant to be camping for the night. It's meant to be tough.'

Gavin smiled. He was looking at Bella fondly and he reached out to touch her hand.

'I am stuffed. Top marks to the chef,' said Bella, holding up her glass. 'It feels so strange having dinner in this house again. Joan cooked me so many dinners here over the years; I used to love visiting her.'

'I know,' said Gavin. 'I felt the same when I first arrived.'

'Come on, let's make a start,' said Bella. She walked over to her bag and pulled out a roll of black bin bags.

'What are the bags for?' asked Gavin.

'Joan and Martin's clothes. I thought we could take them to the charity shop.'

'Good idea.'

They went upstairs to Joan's bedroom.

'Okay, Gavin,' said Bella handing him a bin bag. 'You can clear Martin's wardrobe, and I will tackle Joan's.'

'Sure, but first we need some music.' He walked over to Joan's radio on her bedside table, and immediately cheery songs filled the room. Gavin started to sing along. He was very musical; in the past he would often play Martin's guitar.

Joan had a lot of clothes. Unlike Bella's wardrobe though, Joan's was orderly: the clothes were either neatly folded on the shelves or hanging up. Joan was regularly telling Bella she should tidy her wardrobe so she could find her clothes.

'God,' said Bella, 'I forgot just how tidy Joan was and how many green jumpers she actually had.'

'That's Martin's done,' said Gavin.

'Already!' said Bella as she started to hurry up. Bella had been reminiscing when she saw all her dear friend's clothes again. Joan had always dressed so smartly.

When Joan's wardrobe was cleared, Bella walked over to the wooden dressing table. On top was a rag doll sitting on a small varnished chair made out of clothes pegs. Bella had made the chair at school, especially for Joan. Bella noticed Joan's vintage silver hairbrush and remembered Joan sitting at the table brushing her hair. Joan never wore much makeup and she didn't need to as she was naturally beautiful without it.

'Oh, Bella, the box! Come on, it's just in the spare room.'

Bella saw a large white, plastic box sitting in the corner of the room. She carefully opened it. She knew immediately what was in the box and smiled: Joan's old journals. There must have been over 20.

'What is it?' said Gavin.

'Do you not remember? Joan's notebook and pen on her bedside table.'

'Oh, yes, I remember. I thought it was her shopping list or something,' said Gavin.

Bella continued, 'I asked her what it was one day and she told me a journal she had kept since her dad died. She used to say putting your words on paper helps you to heal and figure out your next steps in life. As you know, she was the only child, and her mum died so young. Joan had a special bond with her dad, and she was absolutely devastated when he died. She told me she felt so lost and depressed without him. They had been through so much together after losing her mum so young.'

'Yes. I remember she talked fondly about her dad. She had so many stories of just the two of them. They worked together and went everywhere together,' said Gavin.

'There is a lovely photo in the sitting room of the two of them on Joan's 21st birthday,' said Bella.

'It was Grace, her friend, the therapist, who introduced her to journaling,' said Bella. 'Grace told Joan that focusing on gratitude would help her through the tough days. The practice would help her focus her mind on the positives in life. Joan looked up to Grace; she was like the older sister she never had.'

Bella pulled out one of the red journals. Opening a page, she started to read and then to laugh.

'What's so funny?' inquired Gavin.

'I see you get a mention here,' said Bella. 'She sent you love.'

'Ah, that's sweet.'

'She also sent Alan love, and Martin got a lot of love too.' Bella started to smile. 'I know what that is about. Remember when you and Alan were having that competition in her garden. Throwing stones to see who could throw them the farthest and as a result, Joan's kitchen window pane got smashed.'

'I remember well,' said Gavin. 'My dad was so angry.'

'Which one of you actually smashed the window?' asked Bella.

'Ah, I can never tell you that, Bella; it's going to my grave.'

'I do have a suspicion it was you,' said Bella laughing.

Bella read on. 'Oh, Joan was grateful to your dad, Sean, for getting the window pane replaced so quickly.'

Bella opened another page and started smiling. 'I'd better put these journals away,' said Bella. 'Otherwise I will stay reading all night.'

'I just had a thought: where is Angel?' asked Gavin. 'Do you need to go home to feed her?'

'No. Angel is okay. Dad said he would call down to her. He likes to escape from my mum sometimes. My house is his little retreat.'

They continued going through the items in each room.

'Bella, if there is anything here you want, apart from all the photos of the O'Sullivans, please take it. I know Joan would love for you to have it.'

'Thanks, Gavin,' said Bella. 'There is one thing I would really love.'

'What is it?' asked Gavin.

'The picture of the white feather in the sitting room. I just love it. Did you know Joan's dad painted it for Joan after her mum died?' said Bella.

'I did,' said Gavin.

'Look,' said Bella, getting excited. 'The old videotapes are still here.'

'Do you remember when Martin got that video camera?' asked Gavin. 'He was going around taking videos of everything and everyone.'

'Christmas 1990,' said Bella excitedly.

'Let's see if we can play it,' said Gavin.

Ten minutes later they were eating popcorn and watching the Kellys and the O'Sullivans having Christmas dinner at Joan's house. Bella was glad the lights were dimmed as her eyes were welling up with tears. They had all been so happy, and it was nice for Bella to see Joan's smiling face again and hear her laugh.

The funny commentary from Gavin as they watched the video saved Bella from needing one of Joan's embroidered handkerchiefs that she had seen earlier in the bedroom. Bella had not laughed as much in a long while; she had forgotten how funny Gavin was.

Bella started to yawn.

'Sorry, Bella, let's get you home. I can see you are wrecked from all the tidying,' said Gavin. 'Thanks for all your help.'

'No problem,' said Bella. 'It was lovely remembering Joan and Martin, sharing stories and watching the old videos with you.'

Bella felt really happy when she got home; she'd had a lovely evening with Gavin. She was honoured Joan had left her journals to her.

Bella's entries in her journal

Three things I am grateful for

Myself

Dinner at Joan's house

Joan's painting of the feather

Joan's wise words to me

Open the door. Don't leave a handsome guy waiting too long.

Go on more dates.

You are too critical of yourself, you must learn to love yourself.

Buy Angel some chew toys.

Putting your words on paper helps you to heal and figure out your next steps in life.

Someone I need to send love to

I send love to Sean for not letting me know sooner about Joan's box for me.

Positive affirmation

I am so happy and grateful that I am surrounded by love. I have met my soulmate and he is kind, caring and respects me.

Chapter 18

Journal entries by an unforgettable friend

*B*ella woke up feeling excited the next morning as she was dying to read some more of Joan's journals. She picked a journal dated 1985 out of the box and started to read.

> *I am so happy and grateful for the O'Sullivans; they are a godsend, my second chance of happiness. They are the family I never had. I love them all so much and they brighten up my days. I would be lost without the joy and laughter they bring to my life. I am truly blessed.*

Bella started to smile. It was so heartwarming to read Joan's words. When Joan's dad passed away, Martin suggested to Joan that they should move from the UK and retire to Ireland. Martin's dad was Irish, and Martin had loved Ireland. Joan was unsure about moving to Ireland at first, but then she realised she had no family left in the UK and a change would be good for them. They decided to move, and after a few weeks of looking, they purchased the small cottage in Galway.

Joan often told Bella the story of how she had got to know the O'Sullivans. One sunny day, Bella's mum was taking her kids for a walk down the road. As they were passing by Joan's cottage, they saw Joan and Martin outside, painting the cottage. Bella's mum stopped to welcome her new neighbours to the village. Joan said it was difficult for her to have a conversation with Veronica as the kids all started asking Joan and Martin questions.

'What are you doing? Why are you painting? What colour is that? What's your name?'

The questions were endless.

'You have white hair; you look like Mrs Claus,' Bella had said.

Elaine was five years old, Bella three, Alan two and Una was only two months old. Alan and Una were sharing the buggy and Elaine and Bella were walking beside their mum. Joan used to chat regularly to the O'Sullivans when they were out walking. Joan got to know them very quickly, and she would have a treat waiting for them. Usually something she had baked especially.

One day Bella's dad knocked on Joan's door. As Joan opened the door, she could see all the kids in the car waving at her.

'Hi, Joan, I know this is a big ask, but would you be able to watch the kids for half an hour this afternoon, please? I need to take Veronica to the doctor, and I have no one else to ask.'

'Certainly. Is Veronica okay?' asked Joan worriedly.

'No, she is really weak,' said Michael. 'I don't know what is wrong with her. I have never seen her so sick; she is in bed for the past two days.'

'I will call over now with you, and see how she is and mind the kids,' said Joan.

When Joan walked into Veronica's bedroom, she knew Veronica would not be able to get out of bed to go to the doctor. She was sweating and looked so pale. Veronica was extremely weak and going in and out of sleep.

'Michael, can you bring me a cold cloth, please?' asked Joan. 'And I think you are going to need to call an ambulance.'

Joan placed the cold cloth on Veronica's forehead. One hour later, the ambulance arrived. 'Go on,' Joan said to Michael. 'Veronica needs you. Don't worry about the kids. I will stay with them.'

Veronica spent one week in the hospital with pneumonia. When Joan minded the kids for Veronica, she absolutely loved it. The kids also loved going to Joan's house.

One evening Joan and Martin were doing their crosswords in the sitting room. For years they would each buy the morning newspaper and sit together doing their crosswords. Bella and her siblings used to love trying to do the crosswords with them. Joan was always encouraging the kids to do the crossword; she said the crossword helped to keep her mind sharp.

'So, Joan, are you minding the kids tomorrow?' asked Martin.

'Yes. Veronica is dropping them around in the morning.'

'I have to say, Joan. I notice a change in you when those kids are around. You just seem so happy. It's good to see you laugh and smile again, Love.'

'Yes, I really do love being with them. They bring such life to the house. They really don't have a care in the world. They make me feel young and alive again. They are the family I never had.'

As Bella continued to read more pages of Joan's journal, she could see it was all about how grateful Joan was for having the O'Sullivans in her life. Bella had not realised how happy her family had made Joan. She could see Joan truly loved them and had a special relationship with each of them. Joan had written in her journal, 'Sometimes, life can surprise you.'

Bella could understand why Joan had left her journals to her. Bella was reminded of the day Joan had picked her up early from school because she was complaining of a pain in her tummy. Joan could tell Bella was anxious about something and was upset. 'Drink up your chicken soup, Bella. It will make you feel better,' Joan had said.

A few minutes later, Bella and Joan were doing the dishes in the kitchen. 'How was school today?' asked Joan.

'I hate school,' said Bella.

'Why, Bella? You loved it last week! Tell me more.'

'Mrs Walsh said my writing is really messy and I should be able to read better for my age. Then today I only got two words correct in my spelling test.' Bella started to cry.

'Bella, don't let what your teacher said upset you like that. It's only a spelling test. Mrs Walsh does not know what you are capable of. Do you want to be a neat writer, read well and get all your spellings correct?' asked Joan.

'I do,' said Bella. 'I want to be clever like you.'

'Well, this is a simple problem to solve. All you need to do is take action and practice these skills.'

'How do I do that?' asked Bella.

'I have a plan,' said Joan. 'Let's write a letter to each other once a week.'

Bella loved writing these weekly letters to Joan and she looked forward to receiving Joan's letters. Bella loved her inspiring words of wisdom and she kept all of Joan's letters. Joan would always end her letters by saying, 'Always remember my wise words; they will guide you through life.'

Together, over some chocolate chip cookies, they would read aloud the letters they had received from each other. Bella loved how Joan gave up her precious time to help her, and Joan's plan had worked.

In the box of journals, Bella found the bundle of letters she had sent to Joan over the years. Reading through them, she could not believe how innocent she had been. She started to laugh as she read more of the letters.

> *Joan, I am never moving out from home or getting married. I am always going to live with my parents.*

As a kid, Bella would never have a sleepover at her friends' houses as she always felt homesick, and her mum would have to collect her. Joan's house, however, was the only exception to this as she felt comfortable at Joan's and regularly invited herself to have a sleepover there. Bella had a special connection with Joan; they were so alike. Joan had been shy and quiet when she was young too, and, like Bella, she never followed the crowd.

The girls were calling around to Bella's for lunch. Angel started to bark.

'It's open,' shouted Bella. 'I'm in the kitchen.'

But when she turned around, she got a surprise. It was Gavin.

'Oh,' said Bella. 'I thought you were my friends. They are calling for lunch.'

'I just popped in with the feather painting; I never gave it to you,' said Gavin.

'Thanks,' said Bella. 'Would you like a coffee?'

'Why not!' said Gavin, sitting down and taking off his coat.

'Have you read all the journals yet?' asked Gavin smiling.

'No, but I am getting through them. They're like a memoir of Joan's life. It was a lovely surprise to receive them.' They chatted until the doorbell rang.

'That must be the girls now.'

Gavin stood up. 'I'd better go, Bella.'

'There is no panic,' said Bella.

'No, I am going to the gym,' insisted Gavin. 'Thanks for the coffee.'

Bella loved how Gavin was so into his fitness. 'Sure. I'll see you later; I still have to collect my car from your house.'

The girls entered the kitchen. Gavin met Laura, Amy, Kate and Sarah. 'It's nice to meet you all. I was just going, I'll leave you all to it.'

As Gavin left, Kate exclaimed, 'Bella O'Sullivan, explain yourself! Who was that?'

Bella laughed. 'My Prince Charming.'

'Who is he?' said Laura.

'You have changed,' said Amy.

'Hang on, girls, it's just Gavin! You probably heard me mention him over the years. He is Martin's grandnephew—Sean's son from Canada.'

'Oh,' said Laura. 'He's the married one.'

The girls all looked disappointed.

'That's such a shame,' said Kate. 'He would have been perfect for you, Bella.'

'Well, he is actually divorced now,' said Bella.

'Really?' said Amy, getting excited.

'Is he on holiday from Canada?' Laura asked.

'No, he has moved to Ireland with work and is living in Joan's cottage.'

'Oh, so he is living quite close to you then,' observed Kate.

'He called over early?' said Laura.

'Yes, he brought me a picture from Joan's house, and then we had a quick coffee before you all arrived,' said Bella, holding up the picture.

'He is very sweet,' said Kate.

'Do you know why he got divorced?' asked Amy.

'He didn't go into the details, but I think his wife may have cheated on him.'

'Poor Gavin,' said Kate.

'So any news?' asked Bella passing a plate of sandwiches around. Kate put out her hand.

'What? I don't believe it!' said Bella. 'Engaged!'

'God, meeting Gavin really threw us off,' said Amy. 'We didn't even notice your ring, Kate.'

'Congrats,' said Laura giving Kate a hug.

'Forget about the tea,' said Bella. 'We need champagne!' She pulled out a bottle from the cupboard. She remembered Joan's words: 'Keep a bottle of champagne handy so you are ready to celebrate when you hear good news.'

'I was saving this for a special occasion,' said Bella. 'This is it!'

Kate was just so happy. She and Matthew had just come back from a weekend in Venice where he proposed.

'It sounds so romantic,' said Bella. 'Any date set for the wedding?'

'No, not yet,' said Kate, 'but we are considering a wedding abroad.'

The time flew by as the girls chatted about weddings.

Bella was so happy for Kate. She had never seen Kate looking so happy either. *A wedding abroad sounds good,* Bella thought, closing her journal and falling asleep.

Bella's entries in her journal

Three things I am grateful for

Gavin

Joan's journals

My friends

Joan's wise words to me

Do crosswords. They will keep your mind sharp.

When you have a problem, take action.

Mrs Walsh does not know what you are capable of.

Keep a bottle of champagne handy.

Life can surprise you.

Someone I need to send love to

I send love to Mrs Walsh for saying my writing was messy and I should be able to read better.

Positive affirmation

I am so happy and grateful that I choose how I react. I exceed in my work, and my dreams come true. I look and feel fabulous.

CHAPTER 19

Prince Charming

The weeks passed by and now it was only two weeks until Christmas. Bella was at the Christmas tree farm when she spotted Gavin in front of her, looking at trees.

'You should get that tree, Gavin. It's perfect.'

Gavin jumped and turned around quickly. 'Oh, Bella, it's you. I was wondering who it was.'

'Sorry, Gavin. I didn't mean to scare you.'

Gavin started to tie a red ribbon around the tree. 'Your timing is perfect, Bella. If you hadn't said anything, I would have been all day deciding on a tree.'

'Any plans tonight, Bella?' asked Gavin.

'Yes, all my nieces and nephews are coming to my house for a sleepover.'

'You're very brave,' said Gavin, 'All five of them for a night. You'll be busy.'

'They are not too much bother,' said Bella. 'Sometimes it's easier when there are more of them as they all just play together. The noise levels can be high though!'

'They are going to be kept busy decorating my tree,' she added with a laugh.

'I haven't seen you around in a while,' Gavin observed.

'I have been extremely busy with work. I got a promotion recently, I am managing a sales team now. It's busy for a while until I settle into my new role,' said Bella.

'Congrats, Bella! Well done; that's excellent news,' said Gavin. 'We must meet up for a drink to celebrate.'

'Sure. I'd better go as I need to cook dinner before the house is invaded.'

'What's on the menu?' asked Gavin.

'Spag bol,' said Bella. 'I could serve them anything. They are always looking to have dinner at my house. They have started to invite themselves around for dinner at this stage.'

'I love cooking,' said Gavin. 'I would cook for you anytime.'

'Oh, the man is just coming there with my tree, Gavin. I'd better go.'

'Enjoy the babysitting,' said Gavin. 'I will text you about that drink.'

'Okay. Bye, Gavin.'

She remembered Joan would say to her, 'You will know if a guy is interested in you as he will persist.'

There was such excitement in Bella's house that evening decorating the tree. Her nieces and nephews put on a little Christmas show for Auntie Bella and Angel, singing all the Christmas songs and dancing. None of them had a dog at home so they adored Angel. One of them was always patting her or bringing her out into the garden to play fetch. They were all full of energy now that they were filled with treats.

The next afternoon when the children left, Bella was wrecked. She could have gone to bed but she had made plans to visit Annie.

On arriving at Annie's, Bella could see Charlie helping James to put up the Christmas lights outside.

Charlie has grown so big. He must be eight now, Bella thought to herself. Just as she stepped out of the car, Annie came out to the front door.

'Save me, please, Bella! These two have been here all day trying to put up the lights.'

'I can see why! You have so many wonderful twinkling colourful lights; your house is so Christmassy.'

'Come into the kitchen, Bella. I have baked some mince pies. How's the house going?' asked Annie.

'Fantastic. It's hard to believe I am nearly three years in the cottage already. I love having my own place.'

'How's Angel?' asked Annie.

'She is big now,' said Bella and started to show her friend some photos.

'She certainly is; she is so adorable. I would love a dog,' said Annie, 'but James doesn't like them.'

'Is there no way to persuade him?' asked Bella.

'Believe me, I have tried,' said Annie.

Annie walked over to the windowsill to get a card while Bella started to dig into a mince pie.

'Here you go,' said Annie. 'It's a congrats card for your promotion.'

'Thanks,' said Bella.

'Are you liking your new management role?'

'Yes, I love it. Working in sales excites me and I am managing a wonderful team. I have learned so much from my manager Ruth. I remember when I advised Ruth I aspired to be a sales manager. She was so supportive and gave me so much encouragement. Management can be challenging at times, but I am embracing it. My journaling is keeping me sane.

'I miss Emma; she is still off on maternity leave.'

'Was it a boy she had?' asked Annie.

'Yes, baby William. The kids are keeping her busy. I will meet up with her over the Christmas break.'

Just then Bella's phone beeped. She looked at the text on her phone and started to smile.

'Who has you smiling like that?' asked Annie looking interested.

'It's just Gavin.'

'Do I know him?'

'I think you met him out one night years ago when we were in college.'

'Oh, I remember him,' said Annie. 'He was over from Canada! Did you not kiss him in that nightclub? Remember we were at that foam party?'

'I did,' said Bella. 'It was just a drunken kiss at the end of the night. That was years ago.'

'Yes, he was flying back to Canada the next day. Well, what did he just say?' asked Annie excitedly.

'He asked if I wanted to go for dinner in town, tomorrow night.'

Annie paused, 'Wait, is he not ...?'

Before she could say it, Bella interrupted. 'No, he's divorced.' She filled Annie in on the details about Gavin's situation.

'So what are you texting back?' inquired Annie.

'I just said "sure sounds good".'

'I think you may like Gavin,' Annie said.

'It's just dinner. We're only friends.'

'Oh, ya, I believe you,' said Annie with a great big smile.

That night when Bella returned home, she went to her wardrobe, looking for a dress to wear for her date the next evening.

God, I have nothing to wear, thought Bella. *That's the worst of it—when you are not going out much in town, you don't buy as many dresses.*

Bella pulled out her old reliable black wrap dress. *This will do, and I will dress it up with my gold sandals and gold bag.*

The next day Bella was busy cleaning her house when her phone rang.

'Hi, Gavin,' she said.

'Hey, Bella. Will I collect you at 7.30pm?'

'Perfect,' said Bella and after a few minutes of chit chat she put down the phone.

Gavin arrived on time and drove them to the Italian restaurant.

Good choice, Bella thought as Gavin opened the restaurant door for her. She remembered Joan's words: 'A gentleman will always open the door for you.' Bella thought the dinner date was perfect. It felt so romantic with the dimmed lighting, the tea lights on the tables, and the soft music playing in the background.

Over the next few months, Bella and Gavin went on several dates and she had a few sleepovers again at Joan's house. It took her a while to get used to Gavin's snoring. She loved the pancakes he would make for her in the mornings. Joan used to always make pancakes for Bella when she stayed over.

One morning, over breakfast, Gavin looked over and blurted out, 'Bella O'Sullivan, I love you.'

Bella was a bit shocked as she was not expecting him to say that.

And she was so used to saying this to herself every morning in front of the mirror that she literally had to stop herself from now saying, *Bella O'Sullivan, I love you,* too.

'You do?' said Bella. 'I suppose I just might love you too,' and she started to smile. Gavin leaned in to kiss her and Bella started to laugh and jumped up from the table.

'What's wrong?' said Gavin.

'Angel was licking my feet,' said Bella.

Gavin laughed. Angel had moved over to his feet now. Bella's phone rang.

'Hi, Mum. Yes, Gavin and I will be home for the roast,' said Bella. She remembered Joan's words: 'Someday, Bella, you will find someone special to take home for your mum's roast.'

Two months later, the postman delivered a letter to Greenfield Cottage.

'Just got it in time,' said Gavin, handing the letter to Bella, 'Angel was about to eat it.'

Bella opened the letter; and smiled. It was a wedding invitation from Kate inviting Bella and Gavin to her wedding in Italy. Bella had finally found her plus-one, and she was delighted it was Gavin. Joan had been right again; he was worth the wait. Bella never imagined herself ending up with Gavin and thought of Joan's words: 'It's not a coincidence. It's the universe at work.'

She was grateful for all those frogs she had met in the past because she could see now how special Gavin was. He was everything Bella had wanted in a man: kind, athletic, and most of all, he respected Bella. He treated Bella like his leading lady.

Bella's entries in her journal

Three things I am grateful for

My job promotion

Gavin

My unforgettable friend Joan

Joan's wise words to me

You will know if a guy is interested in you as he will persist.

A gentleman will always open the door for you.

It's not a coincidence—it's the universe at work.

Wear slippers.

Someday you will find someone special to take home for your mum's roast.

Someone I need to send love to

I send love to Gavin for his snoring.

Positive affirmation

I am so happy and grateful. I have married my Prince Charming and we are living happily ever after.

Epilogue

Bella's entry in her journal

Three magical years have passed by quickly and I am enjoying my forties. Gavin has settled in well to Greenfield Cottage and I have found someone to make me tea again. The kitchen has become the heart of our home. We have started to invite my parents around for the roast. I am grateful for the roast now that my hangover days are behind me.

Angel is still opening doors for me and is comfortably sharing her bed in the kitchen with her new best friend, Jessie the cat.

I am excited as this evening we are calling over to Sean and Audrey's house for their house warming. Gavin's parents have decided to retire to Ireland.

I still keep calling it Joan's cottage and I am so happy that I can still visit the cottage and remember the happy times we all shared there.

Tomorrow my mum is finally taking me wedding dress shopping! While I am shopping for The Dress, Gavin will be busy minding Clare. She has just started walking. Today she said 'Mama' for the first time and I felt so loved and blessed. My dad has offered to lend Gavin a hand tomorrow with the babysitting.

As I write in my journal I am comfortably sitting on a wooden bench in my beautiful garden. I am surrounded by roses, blossom trees and an apple tree, but most of all by love.

I have started to take action on my next goal to become VP of sales. I am so happy and grateful for my wonderful life and my family and friends.

About the author

*M*ary Casey, author of the novel *A home for Bella*, lives in Ireland. Her loyal companion Lucy, a golden Labrador, is always by her side. They enjoy walking together in the beautiful countryside. In her early thirties, Mary felt dissatisfied with life and she was tired of renting. She longed for the freedom of having her own house so she took responsibility and control of her own life.

After successfully purchasing a house, Mary had another burning desire: to write a novel. With this novel she hopes to inspire other single people in Ireland to take action on their dream of homeownership. Mary has also honoured the memory of her unforgettable friend, a gentle soul who always reminded her to have a grateful heart.

Mary holds a bachelor degree in Business Studies and Human Resource Management. She has recently completed a life coaching course, having always been passionate about personal development. She sees the value of self-care and having a growth mindset.

Printed in Great Britain
by Amazon

72560622R00151